Signal
7^{su}

Red
Right
Returning

Red
Right
Returning

ANNE ST. EDMUNDS

ST. MARTINS PRESS ✻ NEW YORK

A THOMAS DUNNE BOOK.
An imprint of St. Martin's Press.

Design by Nancy Resnick

Library of Congress Cataloging-in-Publication Data

St. Edmunds, Anne.
    Red right returning   /   by Anne St. Edmunds.
       p.   cm.
    "A Thomas Dunne book."
    ISBN 0-312-14033-9
    1. Artists—New England—Fiction.   I. Title.
PS3569.T1215R43   1996
813'.54—dc20   95-26260
                                                  CIP

First Edition: April 1996

10 9 8 7 6 5 4 3 2 1

For
Barbara, Chick, Joanne, Lucille, Lucy, Randy, and Tom

Our U.S. Buoyage System is numbered proceeding from the sea. The best way to remember the correct side to pass buoys is *RRR* or *Red Right Returning* to stay in the channel.

—Patrick M. Royce, *Royce's Sailing Illustrated*

Red Right Returning

One

THIS WAS WHERE the plane went down.

Mick Merisi looked overboard at the long graying swells and thought, I shouldn't have come back. What the hell good will it do?

The ferry turned in its course and he sat down on the bench, feeling dizzy. Seasickness, the landlubber's curse.

"Watch what the waves are doing, darling," Claudia used to say. "If you watch them, you can balance yourself with them."

Hearing her voice speaking of waves reminded him of his series of wave paintings. But if the *Wave* series hadn't been such a hit, I would still be holding you.

From the other side of the double bench, he heard a woman sigh. He looked around and saw a girl lying there asleep. A foul weather jacket covered her face and a faded mauve skirt almost covered her legs and bare feet. One dusty Birkenstock sandal slid across the deck as the ferry heeled to starboard.

She looks like an art student, Mick thought.

The girl had long legs like Claudia.

Mick would always remember the first time he saw Claudia.

Her smile! And that face, which looked as though it had stepped down from the walls of the cathedral at Chartres! Yet it wasn't really a smile—her eyes squinted in serene and paradoxical Gothic ecstasy.

It had been a typical London morning with early drizzle. But after more than a year of teaching painting there, Mick had discovered that such early morning gloom was often followed before noon by those racing, jubilant clouds Constable had caught so perfectly. Fresh and wet—God, you could see the man's brush scrambling to catch it, then dancing as fast as the clouds.

She had been looking at the Rubens *Landscape by Moonlight* in the Courtauld. Mick thought she smiled. But was she smiling at him, or at the picture? He couldn't be sure. Did he know her from somewhere? That was impossible—he wouldn't have forgotten her. She had a medieval face, but the kind of modern body Matisse had made such magic of—loose-limbed, with surprising and interesting curves and angles. A body equally at home in luxurious nudity or decked out in some joyously gaudy costume. He couldn't remember what she was wearing. Strange. He certainly remembered everything else.

That afternoon he had gone alone to the Victoria and Albert, as he did whenever he could. Mick usually skipped the endless galleries of decorative arts—that gigantic attic of civilization. Instead, he always went up to the Constable collection, in hopes that he would absorb the brash and arrogant freshness and light of John Constable into his own canvases.

The upstairs gallery was usually empty. But by some miracle the girl from the Courtauld was there that afternoon. No one else—just her. As Mick watched her gaze at a tiny oil on paper that conquered and contained the vast sky (clouds barely touched with Payne's gray and some cobalt blue), he regretted that at the age of thirty-three, he had never yet picked up a girl. He stood next to her until words finally came. "I think a woman who loves Rubens and Constable and looks like you is someone I *should* know, even if I don't."

She turned to him. Her eyes were deep indigo. "Did you know that Constable owned an engraving of that painting? On his deathbed he asked to have his beautiful *Landscape by Moonlight* brought to him. He died with it at his feet, just like one of those stone knights downstairs with his faithful dog. I like that, don't you?" She spoke as though they had known each other forever.

It had all been as simple as that.

Just as simple had been their decision, after they married six weeks later, to go to Dutchman's Island to live and work—Mick on his painting and Claudia on the cookbook she was writing. On that small chunk of New England, far out at sea, Mick had found his own Salisbury plains and marshes.

Claudia had summered on Dutchman's Island with her aunt Betsy every year for as long as she could remember. Betsy LeBrun was rich and single, one of *the* LeBruns. She was also a painter who exhibited regularly in a Newport gallery patronized by rich elderly women. She had given Claudia a good eye for painting and left her considerable property on Dutchman's Island, plus her own share of a substantial trust fund.

The island property consisted of a large house that only in New England would be called a cottage, and a small studio perched out on the high bluffs. Mick and Claudia lived in the studio, renting out the larger house, for like many people born to affluence, Claudia preferred to live with less rather than more. The studio was surrounded by twenty-two acres of moorland and clay cliffs facing the sea. Ancient stone walls crisscrossed the moors and hollows, dipping and rising with the powerful rhythm of a Michelangelo drawing.

Mick had never painted so fluently and well as he did in the two years that passed there. Coming to know the island as he came to know Claudia—coming to love it as she did—had made him see in a way he never had before. Light and water found their way onto his large canvases, translating themselves into color and form. For the first time he truly understood Cézanne's *petite sensation.*

It was in the studio of Dutchman's Island that Mick had painted the *Wave* series. And it was when he was in New York alone, supervising the hanging of them for his first important one-man show, that Claudia found she had to make an emergency visit to the dentist on the mainland . . .

The plane was that damned little four-seater flying Volkswagen, that dinky tin toy Cal Bingham piloted. It served as the taxi all islanders took when in a hurry to reach the mainland. How many times had Cal flown it back and forth for the twenty-minute ride in fog, high winds, and God knows what else? So why had his plane chosen that calm and sunlit day in May, exactly four years and three weeks ago, to drop into the dark sea?

Something swift and silvery broke the surface of the water. A shark. Now was when the big makos came into the bay to feast on basking female swordfish waiting languorously for their lovers. A cormorant surfaced and flew off low over the water.

Mick shivered.

"If I take the plane instead of the ferry, I can still get down this evening," she had said, when he'd telephoned from New York. "But I've got to do something about this tooth. I'm afraid I'll spoil the evening for you by being a terrible grouch—it hurts so much. But I'll be there, don't worry. I wouldn't miss your show, you know that! Do the paintings look wonderful? Oh great! Good luck. I love you so—"

Mick sat shaking his head in despair and disbelief. He'd spent that evening at the gallery clutching the same warm glass of sour white wine and trying to appear more at ease than he was. Finally the last glittering guests and bedraggled students were gone. Four important sales had been made, but Claudia never came.

He had gone to dinner with his dealer and a wealthy collector nibbling on the hook. He had drunk enough good wine, and eaten enough nouvelle something cuisine, to wallow in his triumph. He convinced himself that Claudia's appointment at the dentist must have taken too long for her to catch the Amtrak train. She might still get there; anyway, there would surely be a message from her on his dealer's answering machine. Instead, late that night, at Helen's chic, minimalist loft on Spring Street, Mick had gotten the phone call from Chap Winslow.

He hid his face. Why the hell couldn't he have gone down on the plane with her? They did everything else together—why not die together?

He had spent the last four years wandering, avoiding the island and its memories. He kept hoping that if he couldn't have Claudia, at least he could see again. But how many places had he stumbled numbly through, in the hope that a new motif might mercifully be granted him? For Mick needed to really *see* once more, the way he'd seen the waves breaking when Claudia was alive. The way he'd stopped seeing the day she died.

He looked off toward the horizon. There it was: the sun had vanished into the sea and the small island hung pearly in the distance. The propellers slowed as the ferry entered the channel. A green light at the end of the breakwater blinked steadily. The black and menacing shape of a bell buoy rocked back and forth with the sea, clanging its slow and mournful dirge. A red buoy marking the narrow channel bobbed and swayed as a great black-backed gull landed on it, its yellow beak open to let out the low but authoritative territorial call.

"Mick! Watch where you're going!"

He could hear Claudia's solicitous laughter as she would quickly put her hand over his and man the tiller of her boat.

"Don't you remember? The red buoy should be on the skipper's right entering a channel. Red right returning. Rocks or shallow water are on the other side."

She would kiss him quickly, then squint intently toward the harbor, giving all her attention to tiller and sheet.

Claudia had indeed reminded him more than once of that sailor's maxim whenever she had tried to teach him to sail. But even though the red buoy now lay safely to the right of the boat Mick was on, he reflected that the channel the ferry had just entered seemed far more perilous now than it ever had.

The ferry's deafening horn sounded.

The girl on the bench behind him woke and stretched. She suddenly spun around to tap Mick on the shoulder. "Mr. Merisi! I didn't see you—it's been such a long time! Does Mom know you're coming? She never mentioned it."

"Oh, my God!" he exclaimed. "It's not Cassandra, is it?"

"Uh-huh." She ran barefooted around the bench. "Oh, it's so good to see you!"

Mick could think of nothing to say except, "Hey, I see you got your braces off."

"Yeah, two years ago. No more railroad tracks."

"You must be in college by now—or is it art school?" He remembered Sandy's parents had always been inordinately proud of her artistic abilities.

"Arts and Crafts," she mumbled hastily.

"How do you like it?"

"It's okay," she said without enthusiasm.

In the distance Mick could see the studio. It stood solitary on the bluff like a Hopper lighthouse. Venus dangled in the sky just above the horizon, while on the beach, a dog stood barking at the gently lapping surf. The tide was out and the wet strand of sand glowed darkly.

"Mr. Merisi?" Sandy frowned. "Are you okay?"

"Sorry. I was just thinking of something. What were you saying?"

"Oh, nothing important. You'll see that the island hasn't changed much since you've been gone. I was wondering if you needed a ride?"

"No, thanks anyway. I've got my van."

The ferry tied up at the dock, and they descended the steps to the lower deck where cars were parked.

"Are you planning on staying long?"

Mick shrugged. "I don't know. Maybe a while."

"Oh, look! You've still got Crosby! I'm so glad—Golly, I've really missed her." Sandy's eyes filled with tears as she looked at the cat who lay stretched luxuriously across the driver's seat of

Mick's van, her tail twitching the way it always did when she dreamed her nap would be disturbed.

Mick remembered the night Crosby came to him and Claudia. Her urgent meowing outside the door had interrupted their lovemaking, which had been accompanied by glorious flashes of lightning that split the sky, rain hurling itself against the roof and skylight, and drum rolls of thunder. Mick could still see Claudia's silhouette lit from within and without like a Bonnard as she opened the door and bent down to pick up the kitten, whose pink mouth stretched open in a savage, lonesome cry.

"Look, Mick—she's a calico. See?" Claudia had pointed to the ludicrous orange eyepatch and the one gray tabby paw against all the dripping white fur. "A little patched moon." She had smiled her miraculous smile as she tenderly cradled the wild, wet kitten in her arms, whispering, "I've always wanted a calico cat, haven't you?"

What could he say but yes?

Mick glanced at the lumpy green sleeping bag that lay sprawled across the floor of the van alongside an empty Coke can, a duffel with a broken zipper where a faded sneaker missing its shoelace spilled out, an empty quart container of motor oil, one can of baked beans and another of cat food, a crumpled Milky Way wrapper, an HB pencil, the book on de Hooch Claudia had bought him at the Rijksmuseum that wonderful weekend they'd spent together in Amsterdam, a disposable aluminum roasting pan filled with Kitty Litter, and those rolled-up drawings he hadn't looked at in four years.

"A mess, huh?" he said sheepishly as he picked up the large, limp cat and plopped her down in the back of the van.

Sandy wiped her nose with her yellow sleeve. Mick remembered how she had idolized Claudia. Suddenly he could visualize again the large and awkward child she had been when he last saw her. Penelope and Chap Winslow's kid, the kid Claudia had known from birth.

"It's okay, Sandy," he said helplessly. "Don't cry."

She nodded, and sniffed. "Well, I'll see you later."

Mick waved good-bye absently. Crosby had begun to gag, trying her best to bring up a hairball on his sleeping bag—as she did when she didn't get her own way.

"No, no!" said Mick. "I'm onto you!"

The hairball wasn't ready to come, so the cat leaped up behind him, crying, *"Meeeaaa, rrr, owwww!"*

"Okay! Okay! But stay in your own seat, hear?"

As soon as Mick sat down and turned the key in the ignition, she jumped onto his lap. "Jesus! You damned cat!" The van bumped over the ferry's gangplank.

No one was there to meet the boat. He and Cassandra Winslow had apparently been the only passengers on that evening run. Summer people had yet to begin arriving. Her battered old Subaru (the one Chap used to drive to the Monday morning ferry and back again on Friday night) disappeared around a stone wall as the swollen moon rose over the moor.

Ry Pinkham's grocery store was locked for the night. The young crewmen of the ferry were walking, laughing together, up the road to Mrs. Pinkham's boarding house, where they would sleep until the early morning boat back to the mainland. Water lapping against the ferry tied up at the dock, the bell buoy outside the harbor, and voices growing distant were the only sounds to be heard. Even the gulls had quieted down for the night. A gaff-rigged double-ender was slipping silently into port, its sail mysteriously bright in the dim twilight. Mick recognized Sam Palmer's *Luna*. Nothing had changed, except that Claudia would never meet him at the ferry again, and Cassandra Winslow had grown up.

The van headed toward the high end of the island. The church steeple pierced a few stars in the mauve sky. Wild roses had begun to bloom by the roadside and blackberry blossoms were spangled white among them.

Crosby stood on her hind legs and leaned against the door. She peered eagerly out the open window, her tail twitching with excitement. The smell of the sea was all around, its tangy saltiness blending with roses and brambles in rich perfume. For a split second Mick caught a whiff of the sweet smell of Claudia sleeping.

His hand shook as he turned on the headlight of the van. "We did it, didn't we, Crosby? Yeah, we've come back, girl."

The cat curled up snugly on his lap, closed her eyes, and began to purr.

C H A P T E R

Two

PENELOPE WINSLOW STOOD on her porch framed by glowing cadmium porch lights. "Mick," she called, "Sandy just told me she saw you on the ferry. What a surprise!"

He turned the van into the dirt road that ran past her house to his studio and stopped. She ran toward it. "It's good to see you again, Mick."

Penelope hadn't changed. Claudia had considered her beautiful, but Mick didn't agree. She was small, with reddish-blond hair whose frizzy curls were pulled back primly and held in place by a tortoiseshell barrette. She almost always wore the same type of Madras Bermuda shorts she was wearing now, and the sort of camp shirt Mick felt was best reserved for Boy Scouts and safari leaders. On her feet were white tennis shoes with short socks that had little pom-poms at the heels. She wore large, tinted glasses and her wide smile showed a row of perfect teeth. The smile came easily but had always struck Mick as being somewhat mechanical and artificial. In fact, he'd never understood, in spite of her unquestionable niceness, what Penelope Winslow had in common with Claudia. Yet they had been intimate friends, as well as neighbors.

"I wish you'd written," she said. "It's been such a long time. I wrote to you a while ago at the address you gave me in Santa Fe, but you didn't answer or call. I didn't know how to reach you by phone."

"I've been traveling," he said. Mick wished now he hadn't run into Sandy—that he could have arrived with less fanfare. "I decided it was time to come stay in the studio, for this summer, at least. Get back to work. I'm tired of being on the move."

"I'm sure you are," she murmured.

"Listen, Penelope—I'll just pick up a key from you, if you don't mind. I lost mine somewhere."

Penelope was the only real estate agent on Dutchman's Island. During his absence she had been renting and generally looking out for the property he'd inherited from Claudia. Mick left all the details to her—including signing leases on his behalf and depositing checks in his bank account, after retaining the small commission she didn't want, but he insisted on.

She frowned and pursed her lips thoughtfully. "Well, that's going to be a problem, Mick. You see, I've already rented the studio. The tenant moved in three weeks ago."

Mick rubbed the dark stubble on his chin. He'd been hoping for a shave and shower. "Yeah, of course you would have. I'm sorry I didn't get in touch with you, but I didn't know I was coming back myself until a few days ago."

"It's been four years, Mick," Penelope said gently. She didn't need to add "since Claudia died," but that was implicit in the wounded look she gave him. "When I didn't hear from you, I accepted this man's offer. He loved the place and seemed like he'd be a good tenant. He even offered to pay the whole season's rent in advance. I thought I understood I was to do that whenever possible, unless you told me otherwise. I mean—I *have* rented it the last three summers . . . " Her words trailed off. She sounded awkward and embarrassed, the way her daughter had on the ferry.

Damn. Mick knew there had been some good reason to call Penelope and Chap from time to time. He hadn't been in Santa Fe for more than three months. Her letter was probably sitting in the post office box he'd rented during his stay there.

Crosby meowed.

"Oh poor kitty!" Penelope said. "She sounds hungry. I'll bet you are too, Mick. Come on in. You're welcome to stay in the guest quarters over the garage until we figure out what to do. Mr. Meer—that's the tenant—might be willing to break his lease and move into the Hartley place, although that's a little large for one person, and not quite as secluded. Still, it's not expensive—less than your place." She put her index finger to her upper lip as she contemplated the situation. Then she continued briskly, "Well, I'll talk to him tomorrow. Oh, I forgot! He went to the mainland this morning and I don't think he's back yet. Better still, maybe you should talk to him." She smiled, apparently delighted with this solution. "He's very nice and I imagine he'll be glad to co-operate. If not, we'll think of something. Don't worry." She added quickly, "It's so good to have you back."

He felt the first pang of jealousy at the thought of someone else living in his studio. It had been easier to accept the fact those other summers when he was always thousands of miles away.

Mick parked the van in front of the detached garage and followed Penelope to the house. Crosby darted ahead, tail held high. Strawberries and lettuces, beets, radishes, tomatoes, and purple and yellow pansies were growing in the well-kept garden. Penelope bent down and picked two fat strawberries glowing crimson and scarlet in the twilight. "Remember these?" she said, handing one to Mick, and he recalled that she was famous for her giant strawberries.

The house was exactly as he remembered, crowded with white wicker furniture, faded chintz, braided and hooked rugs, small and daintily patterned wallpaper above white wainscoting, and an endless supply of hand-knitted afghans and needlepoint pillows. There was an upright piano whose top was covered with framed photographs of Sandy at every stage in life, including one

12

of her as small child throwing a beach ball to a teenage Claudia. Mick caught his breath and looked away.

The windows had white curtains whose ruffles only added to the general sense of clutter. Small bottles of colored glass stood in the windows to catch the sunlight. It wasn't much like the austere and uncluttered studio standing on the bluff overlooking the sea. The studio, with Aunt Betsy's few well-chosen pieces of Stickley furniture: those chairs that always looked out on the sea.

"Would you like a drink? Scotch with no ice, right?" Penelope called from the kitchen. "And is leftover tuna okay for Crosby?"

"Yeah, that would be great," he said, feeling suddenly touched that she remembered his usual drink. Maybe it would be good to spend some time around these old friends of Claudia's—

"Goddamn it! Get down!" he yelled, for Crosby had leaped up on top of the piano and was tiptoeing through the photo display.

Penelope rushed in from the kitchen. "What's wrong?"

"Oh, it's just this damned cat. Get down! Get the hell out of here!" Mick picked Crosby up and set her out on the front porch. "Go catch yourself a rat," he said in disgust.

Penelope laughed and brought a tray with a glass of neat Scotch for him and gin and tonic for herself, a wedge of Cheddar cheese, and a basket of crackers. A piece of tuna lay in a blue willow bowl.

"This looks great," Mick said, setting the tuna on the porch for Crosby, who had vanished. He took a long swig of Scotch and sighed comfortably. "So what's up with you and Chap these days?" he asked.

She took a sip of her drink before answering. She didn't look at him when she said, "You really have been out of touch. But I'm sure I wrote you."

"Wrote what?"

"Didn't you know we were divorced? It's almost a year now."

"Jesus!" Mick said. "I didn't know that. God, I'm awfully sorry, Penelope."

She didn't say anything. Mick could hear the grandfather clock ticking loudly as he thought, Why the hell didn't I know that?

13

Funny—he'd always assumed Penelope and Chap had a good marriage, but then, you never know. Chap Winslow had the same sort of pleasant, somewhat artificial friendliness she had—WASP amiability that might have passed for charm with their own sort. They had always seemed perfect for each other. But you never knew what they were *really* thinking . . .

She shrugged. "It's amicable—or at least, as amicable as these things ever are. We were apart most of the time anyway, with him living on the mainland all week. So he's still practicing law there, and I'm still growing my garden and managing properties out here. Not a lot has changed, really."

"Except Cassandra's grown up. She looks great."

Penelope smiled proudly. "Thanks. She's a wonderful kid."

Mick swirled the golden whiskey around in his glass, then tossed it off.

Penelope rose and said, "Well, this sure isn't getting dinner ready. Do you mind eating a little late? Sandy just rushed down to Vinnie's to talk about summer waitress work at the Clam Bar. She'll be back in half an hour or so. Can I make you another drink?"

"No, thanks," Mick said. "If you don't mind, I'd like to walk down to the beach anyway."

He stepped outside and headed down the dirt road toward the shore. It was dark now, but he didn't need to see to find his way. He could have walked this road to the beach in his sleep.

He had already decided to leave in a day or two. But first he just had to take one last look at the studio, although he already knew he couldn't stay. The atmosphere of the island was too filled with Claudia—surrounding him, suffocating him. Even sitting with Penelope had recalled too many of the picnics they all used to have together on the beach . . .

He would speak to her in the morning about selling the property. But not tonight—he was too damned tired. He couldn't remember how many miles he'd driven that day.

A cat's yellow eyes gleamed in the shadows ahead. "Crosby?" Mick called, and whistled to her, but this cat shot across the road, over the stone wall into the dark bayberry thicket. One of those wild ones.

Soon he could hear surf breaking down on the shore. Rounded rocks rumbled as the sea ran out again, rolling them over and over, making them smooth. He made his way through an eroded gully that cut through the low clay cliffs leading down to the beach. He caught his foot and stumbled into a tangle of dried seaweed and nylon fishing line.

He sat down on a driftwood log and watched the moon wobbling restlessly on the surface of the water. It was a Charles Burchfield or Graham Sutherland scene, where every inanimate thing seemed to have acquired a twisted and magical soul visible only by moonlight.

Mick had always felt and dreaded a slight undertow whenever he and Claudia swam here. But the sea never frightened her. She would take him by the hands and coax him into the water, holding him like a child, speaking sweet words of reassurance as they rode the waves together. On a night like this—one of many—she had tempted him in, under just such a moon, and they had ridden the swelling waves, and made salty love on shore under the stars.

Mick buried his face in his hands. Jesus! He had to get out of here.

He stood up to leave, but on the moonlit water he suddenly saw a seal's sleek head surface as it swam along the shore. But it's too late for seals, he thought—you only see them in winter. He sat down again to watch it. In Scotland he had heard some seals were the souls of drowned girls. Selkies, they were called.

The head disappeared under the water. As a large wave broke in close, Mick saw someone ride it in to shore, and then rise majestically from the white foam.

My God, she looks like Claudia, he thought. So tall and slim, long-legged and loose-limbed—lovely. She was nude, too, as Claudia would have been; but as she stepped above the waterline to a dry and sandy spot, Mick saw that she was definitely not Claudia.

15

The girl appeared younger than twenty-seven, the age Claudia had been when she died—probably no more than nineteen or twenty. More than the sea behind her and her nudity reminded Mick of Botticelli's *Venus*. She had the same face.

The girl bent her neck toward the sand and slowly twisted the water out of her long hair, then tossed it behind her. Her neck was long and graceful—like Claudia's, and like the *Venus*. She carefully placed a few stray hairs behind her ears, looking up at the sky as she did. It was a gesture Mick had often seen Claudia make after swimming.

The girl's small and well-formed breasts were outlined by moonlight as she knelt to pick up something from a beach bag lying stranded in the sand. She hung whatever it was around her neck, turned and gazed at Mick, then—to his surprise—walked toward him.

A Hasselblad camera dangled just above her navel, incongruously attached to a cheap, gaudy Guatemalan camera strap. The girl looked down into the ground glass of the expensive camera. Suddenly a brilliant flash of strobe light went off.

"What the hell—" Mick started to say, but she interrupted him.

"Voyeur!" she hissed, then turned and undulated to where her beach bag lay.

Her back was long and straight and her buttocks as smooth and curved as a Brancusi marble. She tossed the camera carelessly down on the sand and pulled out a long, striped T-shirt from the beach bag. She held her arms high over her head and slipped languidly into it, clutching it in folds just above her nipples until it was over her head. She then let it drop to her ankles, smoothing it sensuously over her breasts, her hips and belly, buttocks, and thighs.

Finally satisfied with both the fit of the T-shirt and the feel of herself, the girl picked up the camera, put it around her neck once more, and slung the beach bag over one shoulder. She gazed insouciantly at Mick as she strolled past him.

"Bitch!" he muttered, when he thought she was close enough to hear him. She paused a second, but her only response was an icy smile. Then she continued up the beach alone toward Wrecker's Point, never looking back.

Mick got up and brushed the sand from his jeans. When he turned toward the bluff, he saw the dimly-lit figure of a man who stood at the turn of the beach.

The windows in the studio were dark, but he could see lights in the big cottage across the moor. A growling cat leaped out into the road, startling him. This time it *was* Crosby. She rubbed against his ankles, her fur and tail bristling and erect. Mick picked her up and held her snugly to his chest. She meowed softly.

"Don't be scared. Micky's here," he whispered, scratching her behind the ears as she rode clinging to him, paws on his shoulders, tail twitching.

She licked his cheek with her sandpaper tongue, while keeping an alert watch on the night and the moon and the sea and her wild cousins hiding bright-eyed in the bushes.

Three

"You look like hell, Merisi."

Trudy Glass lay sprawled in a hammock on the wide, curving porch of the cottage, making no attempt to get up when Mick approached her. "I remember when you were pretty as a choirboy. Not now—God, you're a wreck."

"Thanks, Trudy. You're looking good yourself." Mick pulled up a rocker. "How's life these days?"

"A dunghill. What do you expect? Pour me a glass of that, will you?" She gestured toward a crystal decanter of port on the end table. "How about you—have some?"

He poured her a glass of the ruby liquid, thinking of how long he'd known her, ever since his student days. She had been a young and brilliant scholar then, whose special field was the recurrent grotesque in Western art. She'd opened Mick's eyes to *The Book of Kells,* Romanesque carving, Hieronymous Bosch, and Piero di Cosimo with her remarkable and original insights. She had admired his own paintings enough to write a generous and laudatory recommendation for his first fellowship. Over the years she'd invited him to participate in numerous prestigious shows she curated for museums and university galleries. Trudy Glass was a powerful figure in the art world, with the independent wealth necessary to do whatever she wanted, when she wanted. But Mick and Claudia had both noticed her growing addiction to good wine and bad boys.

The last one had been a smug young Belgian from Ghent, some conceptual artist who called himself Marshall Field, after both the French Dadaist and the Chicago department store. His art consisted of obscene practical jokes, happenings performed in fashionable galleries for the glitterati. With Trudy's connections he had become quite famous. Mick remembered seeing him posing with an up-and-coming new model in a recent issue of *Vogue*—the only reading material in some nameless southwestern motel.

"How's what's-his-name?"

She made an impatient gesture of dismissal. "Have you ever heard of Evgeny Otkresta?"

Mick shook his head.

"You will. I met him in Russia last year. You'll be impressed with his work, Merisi. Everyone is."

Trudy raised herself with effort from the hammock. She was wearing a long, loose caftan. Even so, Mick couldn't help noticing her increasing bulk. When she rose to a sitting position, her breathing was wheezy. He thought she was probably not much over fifty, but she seemed years older, puffy and tired.

They went into the sunny living room of Aunt Betsy's elegant cottage. An enormous canvas was leaning against the wall. "Magnificent, isn't it?" Trudy said.

A hammer and sickle were each attached to the center of the canvas with rusty barbed wire that pierced the fabric and twisted around the tools. The same wire also pinned fast the rotting skeleton of a gull just below the sickle's curve. Photographic images were scattered, with seemingly no attempt at composition, around the large surface of the canvas. Mick saw assorted representations of starving children, belly dancers, Callas as *Tosca,* some gorillas placidly munching leaves in a rain forest, World War II Soviet soldiers, Norman Rockwell's famous representation of people praying, a sad-eyed Marcel Proust, a large green parrot, and a recurring number of packages of Chanel No. 5 and Phillips Milk of Magnesia. Some of the photographs had been silk-screened onto handmade watercolor paper, then smeared with fluorescent paint after the manner of Andy Warhol. The largest image was an oval sepia portrait of Lenin, framed with condoms glued to the canvas. Black tar dripped down the entire left side of the painting, while chains and rope drooped from the two top corners. Aluminum spray paint had been used to write words and phrases Mick couldn't read since they were in the Cyrillic alphabet.

Mick knew Trudy expected a comment of some sort—even though she probably knew it wasn't his sort of thing. Hell, he didn't even care for Rauschenberg!

He didn't need to say anything to her, however, for their conversation, such as it had been, was interrupted by the appearance of the artist himself.

Evgeny Otkresta was striking-looking—a combination of Olivier's Hamlet and the young Nureyev. His pallor was enhanced by his all-black outfit: black jeans and motorcycle boots, a black leather vest studded with rhinestones—a thrift shop treasure. Only his long-sleeved brown silk shirt that looked expensive broke the black and white.

A Velázquez palette, Mick thought. Except he's probably never heard of the great Spaniard.

"Darling," said Trudy. "I'd like you to meet Mick Merisi, who's not only a superb painter himself—remember, I included him in the piece I wrote for *transitions?* He's also our landlord, and he's just been admiring *Homage to Vladimir Ilyich.*"

The artist glanced at Mick and said, "So?"

"It's very full," Mick mumbled. "I think I'd like to look at it some more . . . "

Evgeny turned to Trudy and began gesticulating wildly while shouting at her in Russian.

"Of course." She patted his cheek. "I'm sorry. Of course, I should have thought—" She turned to Mick. "He's not ready to show it yet. I'm afraid it upset him for you to see it."

"That's okay." Mick attempted a friendly smile at Evgeny. "I understand. I usually feel that way myself about a work-in-progress." He noticed beads of sweat on the young Russian's forehead, although the day was not excessively hot.

As soon as they were out on the porch again, Trudy whispered, "He's so terribly sensitive about his work—awfully private. Still, I'm hoping he'll let MOMA take a look at it soon. They're interested—very interested. It's such a damned important work! Of course, he's still got a former Soviet dissident's fear of someone reporting on him. God, I tell you, Merisi, you and I will never know what courage is!"

Mick said good-bye and walked down the road toward the beach. A storm the night before had left the air sparkling. Everything shimmered.

Claudia had loved mornings such as this. Mick thought of her joyous early awakening to such a day. "Oh, what a morning this is going to be! Touch me, Mick—touch me!" she would whisper as she tossed off the sheets and spread her silky thighs to catch the rays of dawn that shone on her: a vision like Titian's glorious *Danae* welcoming her lover as a heaven-sent shower of gold.

A dog barked, jolting him back to reality. A child about nine years old ran toward Mick, calling, "Stubbs! Come back here, Stubbs!"

A Welsh Corgi came racing on short legs toward Mick. As soon as he reached him, the dog flipped over and rolled happily in a large puddle. Then he jumped up, put his muddy paws on Mick's legs, and barked urgently.

"Hey! Grab him, mister!" the child yelled. While Mick held the dog, she fastened a leash to his collar. When it was attached, she shook her finger, saying, "Bad Stubbs! Bad dog!" She glanced at Mick. "I'll bet you have a cat. Do you?"

Mick nodded.

"I figured. He goes crazy over anyone who's got a cat. That's why he ran off."

"Is he yours?"

"No. He belongs to Mr. Meer. He lives over there." She pointed toward the studio. "But I'm taking care of him while he's over on the mainland. He pays me to," she added proudly.

"Well, I can see you do take very good care of Stubbs." He put out his hand to the child. "I'm Mick Merisi. I happen to own the studio Mr. Meer is renting. What's your name?"

"Cathy Girtin. I live at Blackberry Farm."

"Then you must be Tom and Angie Girtin's granddaughter."

"You know them?"

"Sure, we were neighbors."

Poor little kid, he thought. Mick remembered the scandal, five years earlier, when the child's mother ran off with some radical environmentalist wintering on the island. Her father had gone to work off his grief and anger on a trawler that went to sea for weeks at a time, leaving his child indefinitely in his elderly and eccentric parents' care.

"Stubbs is usually a real good dog—except when someone's around who's got a cat. Like I said, he's crazy then." She pulled at the leash, "Well, I'll be seeing you around. Come on, Stubbs."

On the rise behind the stone wall, Mick could see Evgeny Otkresta pacing up and down the lawn by the boathouse. He took deep drags on a cigarette and looked impatiently out to sea.

Mick suddenly wondered if it hadn't been the Russian artist he'd seen waiting in the shadows of the bluff for the strange girl with the Hasselblad. "Poor Trudy," he muttered. "Hell, poor little kid, poor me. Poor everybody—"

He continued down the road to the beach.

The water was an intense and dazzling Prussian blue. It seemed to have been washed and shined bright by the storm. Mick looked out to the horizon, remembering another day just like this when he'd returned home after a trip to the art store on the mainland.

He'd gone down to the beach to find her. Claudia was sailing *Felicity*. The frisky little wooden catboat sliced the rippling waves with her radiant at the helm. The great white sail formed a perfect angle and slashing line against the background of pale cerulean sky. Air, light, and sea had been a Normandy Channel painting by Monet. Seeing it, Mick felt compelled to do Monet (or Manet, for that matter) one better. The painting he began that day—a damned good one—was still hanging on the wall of the studio, over the dining table. Claudia had refused to let him sell it.

He suddenly needed to look inside the studio, to see it again. When he'd done that, Mick felt certain he'd be able to leave Dutchman's Island for good, sell the property, never come back again. But he had to force himself to look at the studio first.

He was glad the tenant wasn't there and hadn't bothered to pull the curtains in his absence. When Mick peered in the window from the deck, he almost didn't recognize the room. The Stickley chairs were covered with dark green chenille throws. The kilim rug he and Claudia had brought back from London, their wedding gift to each other, had been replaced by one of those dingy, multicolored braid rugs he'd noticed Penelope was excessively fond of. The Amish quilt was gone, too. The bed was now covered with a white bedspread whose fringe had come partially unraveled, probably by Stubbs. In place of Mick's paintings a few framed marine studies from the gift shop in town were hung. They looked pathetically small and wrong on the high walls of the studio. One of them—a lighthouse—was tipped lopsided on the wall next to the kitchen, Claudia's kitchen.

Even his easel was gone.

Mick's first response was anger at Penelope. What the hell right had she to remove his things—Claudia's things? But right away, he felt ashamed, thinking of the kindness she and Sandy had shown him in the two days he'd been back. She'd only been looking out for those possessions she knew had been dear to Claudia.

He reminded himself that Penelope, too, had loved her.

Mr. Meer appeared to be a carver of decoys. The dining table was covered with newspaper and a partially carved figure of a bird rested there. An old-fashioned wooden toolbox filled with gouges, chisels, sandpaper, and glue stood next to it. An unplugged burning iron lay next to the toolbox and a few glass eyes were scattered around. One finished decoy perched on the windowsill by the bed. Mick recognized it as the unique variety of tern that nested up the beach a ways at Wrecker's Point. It was a good likeness, he admitted. Not bad, if you liked that sort of thing.

He had seen enough. He walked down the beach toward Wrecker's Point, making a mental list of all the things he'd have to discuss with Penelope before he left for good. Where she had put his paintings, for example.

He followed the tideline out toward the long spit of land that was Wrecker's Point. Years ago, Tom Girtin, the elderly farmer whose land included the dunes, had appointed himself solitary keeper of the rare terns that nested there. He was known to sometimes materialize silently and abruptly among the sand mountains, holding a shotgun, indicating to any intruders they had better leave before they disturbed the screaming birds. Mick had no desire to walk into the dunes, but no one would care if he continued along the shore below the tideline.

He didn't know why he wanted to go there—he just did. He had often walked there with Claudia.

He turned around the spit of sand, where the dangerous cross-chop of bay and ocean met. The west beach at Wrecker's Point was the best place on the island for beachcombing—the place where, for reasons having to do with the force of the waves and the pull of the tides, the sea constantly tossed up great piles of flotsam and jetsam.

Claudia had loved to search among those shattered wrecks of dinghies, oars, lobster traps and buoys, nylon line, summer furniture, bottles, cans, seashells, utility poles, and God knows what sort of thing for something only she would find precious. For her, the mess after each storm or moon tide always yielded up something worth keeping.

No one ever swam there because of the lethal currents, but Mick noticed some lovers who were already meeting on the sandy spit, even though it wasn't yet summertime. College kids who swarmed to the island for summer work, sun, and windsurfing sometimes went to Wrecker's Point seeking privacy, in spite of the possibility of old man Girtin surprising them in the act.

The girl lay on her side just below the litter piled on the beach, her back to Mick. He assumed she faced someone hidden by the curve of her shoulders and hips. He looked up into the dunes to see if he could make a discreet exit and continue on his way, but then realized the girl was alone. She was perfectly still in the wet sand.

"Oh God!" Mick whispered. He ran toward her, loudly calling her name, stumbling as he ran.

Suddenly he stopped. No, of course it couldn't be Claudia, not dressed in old cut-off faded jeans like that. After all, she had been planning on going to his opening. She would have wanted to look her best. The bronze-colored silk dress he had helped her choose at Barney's had been missing from the closet. She would only have worn that, and her grandmother's diamond earrings to frame her lovely, regal face.

No, this wasn't Claudia.

As Mick approached the girl lying in the sand, he suddenly knew that neither he nor anyone else could ever disturb her perfect stillness.

A pair of terns floated nonchalantly on the water, while others circled screaming above him. He touched the girl's bare shoulder. It was stiff and cold. When he went around to the other side to face her, he saw fading blue eyes that stared at nothing. Her long wet hair lay limply draped across her mouth and neck. Slippery kelp and bubbles of green rockweed twisted and trailed through it, making her resemble the famous Sir John Everett

Millais portrait of the drowned Ophelia. Her cut-off jeans were unzipped. A faded red tank top revealed she wore no bra. Her feet were bare and her legs were long and graceful. The outgoing tide lapped gently at her toes.

"Oh my God," Mick whispered again. He recognized the girl with the Hasselblad.

Except the camera was no longer around her neck.

Four

MICK LOOKED AT the girl's body again. What if it was gone after he finally got to the farmhouse where he could telephone Jerry Francis, the only policeman on the island?

It was a long hike to Tom Girtin's place from the dunes. He had no idea as to how the body might vanish—unless the same current that had carried it in could also carry it out again. The fear stayed with him as he struggled up the first hill of sand that slithered out from under him with every step. He hadn't realized he was that out of shape; all that sitting in the van and driving one goddamned place after another . . .

He heard someone singing. God, did kids still listen to the Beach Boys? For it was certainly some child's high voice he could hear singing over the loud cries of terns wheeling and screeching above him, swooping toward him with their sharp beaks—and the cheeping of small downy ones with fragments of eggshell still stuck to their feathers.

Cathy Girtin peered down at him from the top of the dune. "Hey, Mr. Merisi! You'd better get out of there before Grandpa catches you!"

"Cathy! Run and tell your grandpa to call the police. There's been an accident. Someone's hurt—hurry!"

She hesitated. "I can't."

"Why not?"

"Because I'll get into trouble. I'm not allowed here. You're not, either."

"Listen to me, Cathy. This is important. Just go! I'll think of some excuse for you, I promise. I'll take all the blame."

"You're sure?" She frowned skeptically.

"Yes, I'm sure, damn it! Just hurry!"

He watched the child disappear behind the dune. He climbed to the crest of the sandhill and watched her walk slowly and reluctantly toward the farm. A red bandanna drooped from the back pocket of her cut-off jeans—the same type of shorts the dead girl wore. It seemed to Mick Cathy was walking as slowly as she possibly could, but finally he saw her small figure go in the back door of the distant farmhouse. Then he returned to the beach.

The tide was further out now. Water no longer lapped at the dead girl's feet. It looked as though she must have washed ashore on a large breaker—all that seaweed in her hair. It was crazy to swim out here, she must have known that. Everyone else did.

But why was she swimming with her clothes still on? She hadn't worn any the other night. And why was her fly unzipped?

Mick felt dizzy and sick. He knew for certain, at exactly that moment, that someone had killed her.

He visualized her as she rose from the sea the other night. She had been lovely, no doubt about that. Yet something about her— her arrogance it was—invited anger, too. She looked younger now than she had that night, although perhaps it was only the childish clothes she was wearing. Who was she, anyway? Perhaps someone he didn't recognize because she'd been only a child when he last saw her? After all, he hadn't recognized Cassandra Winslow at first, when he saw her on the ferry, and he had known her well. Someone that age could change a lot in four years.

He watched the sun climb higher. Terns dived into the sea, as though it were a morning like any other. Offshore he saw the *Luna* sailing as she had been the night he arrived. On the distant horizon was another sailboat whose lines he didn't recognize. The ferry was steaming toward the mainland and a small plane droned lazily overhead. Up by the cottage a kite was flying—a flash of scarlet joyously dipping and diving in the breeze.

Mick supposed it was Sandy flying the kite, until he remembered being awakened that morning by her car starting up. She'd been wearing a black rubber wet suit as she fastened her windsurfing board to the rack on top of the car. She was probably still sailing, for it was a perfect day—the wind light but fresh. He was glad she wasn't around. He suddenly felt protective of her, frightened for her, as though he had inherited Claudia's concern for the child she had once taken care of. Sandy was about the same age, height, weight, and general coloring as this girl who had been killed by someone. Someone who was probably still on the island.

Was it really Trudy's house guest he'd seen on the beach the other night? Hell, it could have been anyone standing there in the shadows, away from the bright moonlight. Mick didn't want to think it was Evgeny Otkresta, with his quick temper and nearness to Sandy.

His eyes fixed on anything other than the body lying in the sun with flies swarming around it. He took off his sneakers and walked away to the water's edge on the other side of the sandspit. The cold sea stung his ankles.

Mick cupped his hands, then turned and walked back to the girl's body. He dripped the water he was holding onto it—looking away as he did. He made trip after trip to the edge of the sea, always returning to sprinkle her body with water, as though he were some cloistered monk performing a sacred ritual whose meaning he didn't comprehend but whose importance he didn't question.

Something cold and slimy splashed against his leg. It was the large carcass of a silvery fish—chunks of flesh chewed away—swishing round-eyed and open-mouthed in the bubbly froth.

Mick picked the fish up by the tail and angrily hurled it out to sea. It reminded him of all the unseen dangers beneath the bright surface of the water.

He took off his shirt and covered the girl's face. Far off, he heard a siren wail. At the bend of the road, just after the cottage, he saw the blue flashing lights of a police car. Then Mick sat down at the water's edge to wait.

He had no idea how long he'd been sitting there when Jerry Francis stood behind him. "So it's you, Merisi. What's going on here?"

Tom Girtin and his granddaughter were with him.

Mick pointed to the body without speaking. Jabbering passed back and forth on a police radio—voices competing with static. Jerry spoke over the walkie-talkie in numbers and letters, gibberish that meant nothing to him.

"Okay," the policeman said. "Get the kid the hell out of here, Tom. You better go, too."

He held a Masonite clipboard. A walkie-talkie jutted from his rear pocket and a black pistol and billy stick hung from his thick waist. He walked over to the body and yanked Mick's blue chambray workshirt from her face. "Was this here when you found her?"

Mick shook his head. "No, it's mine."

"Listen, Merisi," Jerry snapped. "What the hell else did you change? You're not supposed to touch a thing, not one single goddamned thing, you know. That's tampering with evidence," he added, dramatic menace in his tone.

"She was getting dry. The sun's so damned hot. And the flies—" Mick gagged and couldn't speak.

"What time did you get here?"

"I don't know."

Jerry glanced at Mick's wrist. "You're wearing a watch. Don't you ever look at it?"

"Sometimes, but I guess I haven't for a while. Does it matter?"

"On a police report it sure as hell does." Jerry began to write energetically on the clipboard, now and then kneeling beside the girl's body, touching her.

"Did she drown?" Mick asked.

The policeman lifted a lock of the girl's long hair, and hesitated before speaking. "Sure doesn't look that way to me."

"Who is she?"

"Never saw her before in my life. You know how it is, Merisi— summer brings a hell of a lot of new faces from all over the place out here. I take it you don't know her, then?" Jerry didn't look up as he wrote on the clipboard.

Mick wondered if he should volunteer any information about seeing the girl two nights before, but decided to wait until he was asked. "No, I don't know her," he said. He watched Jerry stroll around the body, making numerous notes. "What will you do with her?"

"I've radioed the pathology guys. They ought to be here soon."

The flies returned. A large bluebottle settled on the girl's wrist, buzzing loudly. Jerry ignored it, but Mick couldn't stop staring at it. Finally he said, gesturing toward the fly, "Can't you get that thing off her?"

"What thing? Oh, yeah." Jerry flicked his finger at the fly, but it only flew up to her cold cheek. Its buzzing grew louder. The air was abruptly disturbed as a sudden gust of wind came up. But it wasn't wind Mick felt and it wasn't the fly he heard now.

A helicopter landed on the small strip of beach, scattering sand and broken seashells. A paramedic jumped out even before the noisy propeller stopped. A police photographer joined her and began snapping flash pictures as the paramedic knelt beside the body, felt for a pulse, pulled a stethoscope from her back pocket, and listened.

Finally she nodded to her partner.

More flashbulbs went off. A policeman with a video camera shoved Mick aside, saying, "I need some room here."

A slight, balding man in a gray suit stood talking earnestly with Jerry Francis, who soon pointed to Mick, then to the shirt he held in his hand. Mick had noticed Jerry seemed surprised, even annoyed, to see the man when he'd stepped out of the helicopter. They obviously knew each other. He suspected that Jerry was defending his removal of the shirt, for he shook it and pointed to it emphatically, then to the girl again, then to Mick. Mick felt that he and the dead girl had both become objects, dehumanized, props in some theater of the grotesque and absurd.

The man walked away from Jerry and strolled lackadaisically around the girl's body. All the people working around her stood back while he looked at her. He was just looking—but Mick could tell he was looking hard, the way a painter does. He knew he was searching for that telling detail that could pull the whole composition together.

The man soon turned and nodded to Jerry, then came over to Mick and offered his hand. He spoke quietly, with a pronounced Providence accent. "I'm Antoine Caron, Detective Division, State Police. Mr. Merisi?"

"How do you do?" Mick mumbled. Caron didn't look like a cop—no badges, no gun, nothing. He was probably French-Canadian, like so many New England police. With a name like that, he had to be, Mick guessed. But he didn't look like one—so slight and fair-skinned.

"Fine, thanks. Mr. Merisi, I'd appreciate it if you could tell me everything you can about finding her. By the way, you didn't move the body, did you?"

Mick shook his head and once more explained as much as he could. He realized there was little to tell. He'd been walking on the beach, and there she was—just like that. Dead.

Caron listened attentively, saying nothing. He squinted his eyes from the afternoon sun, but nevertheless tried to maintain eye contact with Mick. "What were you doing here?" he asked, but his tone wasn't that of an interrogator, not at all. It was more like the polite but bored and essentially disinterested small talk strangers usually made at cocktail parties.

"I own some property on the island. I've been away for four years, but I came back two days ago to put my property on the market. My own house, my studio, that is, is rented, so I'm staying with some friends." Mick slapped at the bluebottle fly now buzzing around his bare chest. "I'm sure Captain Francis remembers me from when my wife was killed in a plane crash between here and the mainland, four years ago. He did a lot of looking into that." Mick had never forgotten or forgiven the callous treatment he'd received from Jerry at that time, the painful and unnecessary questions he'd been asked.

He paused and looked down at the sand. He noticed his feet were bare and wondered where his sneakers were.

Then he heard Caron speaking softly and sympathetically. "I'm sorry to hear that. Under those circumstances this must be even more distressing for you than it normally would be. Please accept my apologies for having to ask so many questions. I'll try to be quick."

Mick nodded. For a moment he almost admitted to this stranger he'd even thought the girl was Claudia.

Caron said nothing more for what seemed a long time; just stood and gazed thoughtfully at the body. Then he looked up into the dunes, down the beach in the direction Mick had come, and finally said, "Mr. Merisi, I appreciate what you've told me, but I'm afraid I still don't understand what you were doing here on this beach, right here, at this very spot."

"I don't know. Just walking up the beach." Mick took a deep breath. "To tell you the truth, I haven't any idea why I came this way, but I sure wish to hell I hadn't. There's a bird sanctuary up there in the dunes." He gestured in the direction of them. "Tom Girtin, the farmer who owns the land behind the beach, gets pretty damned skittish about anyone trespassing in there. I guess that's why I stayed down by the water's edge and saw her—just to keep out of the nesting area. I thought it was a couple of kids making out at first. They do that out here, everyone knows that. But then I saw she was alone—"

Mick suddenly thought he'd said a stupid thing. He wondered if he hadn't made himself out to be some sort of voyeur, exactly what the girl had taken him for the other night. Oh, Christ, there was a hell of a lot he was going to have to explain. Why was he feeling this way, anyway, as though he were guilty of something more than being the unlucky son-of-a-bitch who discovered a corpse on a beautiful day down by the sea? Something about Caron's calm manner made Mick more apprehensive than Jerry's aggressive surliness had.

"What do you mean, 'pretty skittish'?" Caron asked.

"Just that. He doesn't like trespassers. He's afraid they'll keep the birds from nesting, I guess."

"I see. And what did you do while you were waiting for Captain Francis? Do you remember?"

Mick suddenly remembered reading somewhere that police knew the murderer was often the first person at the scene of the crime, was often someone who appeared eager to help the police—someone too full of curiosity about the case. It was in a book about the Leopold and Loeb case—that's where he'd read it—the Loeb boy's eagerness to be part of the act had alerted the police, made them suspect him.

"Mr. Merisi?" Caron was waiting for an answer.

"What? Here? I just waited." He remembered the discussion between Caron and Jerry about his shirt. Better fill him in. "No, that's not quite true. She was wet at first—I think—when I first got here. I guess she'd been in the water. Then she started to dry off and there were flies swarming all over her. It was hot, so I sprinkled her with some water."

"Did you touch her?"

"No."

"How did you know she was wet if you didn't touch her?"

Mick was puzzled. How the hell had he known that, anyway? Then he remembered. "Her hair. That's right—that's what it was. Her hair looked wet."

The detective nodded. "But you did take off your shirt and cover her face with it, am I correct?"

"That's right."

"You're absolutely certain that's all you did?"

God, how he wanted to get away from there! Mick suddenly

wondered if Penelope was home. He thought it would be pleasant to sit in the kitchen and share a pot of tea with her; it would taste better than Scotch, at this moment. Claudia always said Penelope made the best tea in the world . . .

"Yes, that's all. I started to leave, to go somewhere and call Jerry—Captain Francis—but then I saw the kid—Tom Girtin's granddaughter—up in the dunes. I told her to go back to the house and ask Tom to phone the police. That's about it."

"So a child was here with you?"

"No. I mean, I don't know. I didn't see her anywhere around until I was up in the dunes. I guess she was playing up there somewhere."

"Alone?"

"I guess so. She had a dog with her earlier, but he didn't seem to be around any longer."

"So you saw the child earlier?"

"Yes, when her dog got away. Well, the dog's not actually hers—she's taking care of it for someone."

Oh, hell, what did I say all that for? Mick wondered, but Caron said nothing. He looked at his watch, as though he was late for an appointment, then studied his perfect, clean fingernails.

"You don't think she drowned, do you?" Mick said quietly.

Caron looked away from him toward the body. "There's no telling the cause of death at this point. I wouldn't speculate on it. We'll have to wait and see what pathology determines." He changed the subject. "Excuse me, did you say you didn't know her?"

"Right." Mick hoped the detective wouldn't ask him if he'd ever seen her before.

Their conversation was interrupted when Jerry came over, holding Mick's shirt. There were splotches of paint on it. Mick noticed a couple of smears of alizarin that might have passed for blood. "How about this? Do we need it?"

Caron sighed. Even Mick had guessed they would keep his shirt as evidence of some sort. "Sure. Give it to them." He gestured absently toward the helicopter.

One of the policemen came over and handed him some Polaroid pictures. Mick looked away. He didn't want to see the girl's
blank eyes again. Ever.

Caron shuffled through the pictures, his face expressionless.
"Jerry, I guess you'll be needing some of these. You'll get some
up there, too, won't you, Dave?" He pointed to the dunes, and
the photographer nodded and headed toward them.

"No ID, huh?" Jerry asked.

"Not on her." Caron handed him a picture, then casually
stuffed the others in his jacket pocket, as though they were pictures of the new baby to show the guys at the office. He held out
his hand to Mick. "Thank you so much, Mr. Merisi. You've
been a great help."

He removed some sort of measuring device from his trouser
pocket and began to pace the area several yards around the body,
stopping now and then to write in a small black loose-leaf notebook.

Mick noticed that a large area had been cordoned off around
the body and up into the dunes with stakes and red plastic ribbon. The ribbon was printed with bold, black lettering that read:
"POLICE. KEEP OUT." He saw his sneakers lying on the sand behind the helicopter and started to wander over to put them on.

Caron glanced at him, then at Jerry Francis, but continued jotting down notes.

"What do you think, Tony?" Mick overheard Jerry say. "Got
enough?"

"I think he'd better go back with you, Jerry. Get a full report,"
Caron replied.

"Gotcha, boy!" Jerry replied, convincing Mick the two men
knew each other well.

He motioned to Mick to lead the way through the dunes.

Caron followed them. "Jerry," he said. Mick continued walking ahead but overheard Caron say quietly, "Listen, I'd appreciate it if you'd take it easy."

"No problem."

Caron turned and went back to the body.

36

When they reached the police car parked off the dirt road that led to Blackberry Farm, Mick watched the helicopter rise into the sky, its propeller clattering over the sound of the screaming terns. As soon as it grew small and silent, vanishing toward the mainland, another one landed on the beach.

"Looks like they're planning to stay awhile," Mick commented.

Jerry grunted officiously as he opened the car door. "Yep, sure looks that way. Come on—let's get going."

Where the hell was that Hasselblad? Mick wondered. When Caron found the girl's camera, and somehow he didn't doubt the detective would, he'd probably find film inside it. Film that, when developed, would reveal Mick's own image sitting alone and staring at her on the beach by moonlight.

Once again he asked himself why he'd ever come back.

Five

JERRY SAT DOWN at his desk in the small room in the firehouse which served as police headquarters. "You say you never saw her before?"

"No, I didn't say that," Mick replied.

"What are you telling me, Merisi? I thought you said earlier this afternoon you didn't know her."

"I don't—I mean, I didn't. But I had seen her once before."

Jerry said nothing. Instead, he got up from his desk, opened the door, and snapped his fingers impatiently. "George, come here, will you?"

An obese young man wearing a dark blue fireman's uniform strolled in. "What do you want now?" he asked.

Jerry gestured toward a chair in the corner of the office. "I've got a couple of questions to ask my friend Mr. Merisi here. I'd appreciate it if you'd join us—sit in on our conversation for a few minutes. You know what I mean. Won't take long."

George picked up a coffee-stained copy of *Time* and thumbed diffidently through it. The point of Jerry's ballpoint pen clicked out and he began writing again. He didn't look up at Mick as he tossed the Polaroid of the dead girl across the desk. "Now, tell me exactly when and where you saw her prior to today."

Mick turned away from the photograph. "The night I arrived here. She was swimming off the beach in front of my studio."

"What night was that?"

"Tuesday."

"Tuesday of this week?" Jerry wrote rapidly soon turning the page back to expose a fresh sheet of paper.

"Yes." Strange, how it seemed so much longer ago than that.

"Were you alone?"

"Yes."

Jerry's lips were a thin, hard line. He put his pen down and looked intently at Mick. "Look, Merisi, I want you to give me the whole story this time. And I'm advising you, for your own sake: don't leave anything out. I mean anything—nothing, *nada*—you understand?"

"Sure, Jerry. I understand."

"Now, did you or did you not speak to her?"

"No. I mean, yes—I suppose I did."

"Okay, so it's yes. What did you say? Exactly."

Mick felt vulnerable sitting there with two men in uniform, and himself without a shirt. His strange meeting with the girl had become much more than absurd in the light of what happened. It was grotesque, obscene, terrifying. "It doesn't matter," he mumbled. "I didn't say anything, really."

"Merisi, that's for me to decide. Either you said something or you didn't. What was it? 'Hello, good-bye, what's your name?' Let's have a straight answer."

Mick wriggled in his chair. It felt sticky. "Bitch," he murmured.

"Bitch, did you say? That's an interesting icebreaker, I must say. Would you mind telling me *why* you said that to her, for Christ's sake?"

"She took my picture and I didn't want her to."

"I thought you said it was dark. How the hell did she take your picture, then? Anyway, how are you so sure it was the same girl? What was she wearing—same outfit as today?"

"No, nothing. I mean she wasn't wearing anything."

George gave out a long wolf whistle and slapped his thigh.

"Get a grip on yourself, will you, George?" Jerry snapped. "Continue, Merisi."

"I'm absolutely certain it's the same girl. She is—she was—distinctive-looking. She didn't look like anyone else. . . . " Except Claudia. "There was something about the shape of her face, her eyes, her long arms and legs. Everything about her. I thought she looked like the nude in Botticelli's *Birth of Venus*."

"What the hell's that?"

"A famous Renaissance painting. She was able to take my picture because she had a strobe light on her camera."

Jerry tilted back in his chair and touched the tips of his fingers together, forming a cathedral. He brought his fingertips to his lips, mused a moment before speaking quietly and pompously this time. "I don't understand what you're saying, Merisi. Am I to understand that this girl"—he gestured toward the Polaroid—"quite an attractive girl at that, was swimming nude and alone at night on your own property, yet you made no overtures whatsoever to her, except to call her 'bitch,' even though she was a total stranger?" His voice grew louder. "Even though she herself apparently felt sufficiently at ease with you to take a photograph of you?"

He rose and leaned toward Mick, his knuckles white and bony from the weight of his body resting upon them. "I'd like to know what the hell you were doing on the beach that night, anyway. It sounds to me like you're leaving something out—and I want to know what it is. Don't hedge on me, now, Merisi. I'm warning you!"

"I'm not. Believe me, Jerry, I'm not. I have no reason to," replied Mick, wearily. "I'm telling you exactly what happened. I went down there because I hadn't seen the beach for a long time—no other reason. It had just turned dark and I had a little time before dinner. The moon was full and shining brightly off the water, so I got a pretty good look at her. She was swimming alone, nude, skinny-dipping, whatever you want to call it. At first I thought it was a seal I saw out there. But then this girl came out of the water, hung a camera around her neck, walked up to where I was sitting, snapped my picture, and called me a voyeur—not a name I appreciate being called."

Jerry said nothing until Mick spoke again. "Well, maybe I *had* been staring at her, but it still struck me as kind of a kinky thing to do."

"So what happened next?" Mick was aware that now George was watching him, spellbound by his tale.

"She put on a long, striped T-shirt, then walked away, real slow, toward Wrecker's Point. I never saw her again until I found her lying there today."

Mick's legs ached and his left foot had fallen asleep. He wanted to get up and walk around, walk out of there, but instead, he only shook his leg vigorously. "Usually no one swims off that beach, especially at night—although I'll admit my wife and I used to, often. I was surprised to see anyone else there. It was a shock."

He didn't add "because at first I thought she looked like Claudia."

Jerry smirked, and sat down again. Slowly and deliberately he studied the ins and outs and possible functions of a bent paper clip he had picked up from the pile of junk littering his desk before deciding cleaning his fingernails was the best use he could put it to. He proceeded to do so, carefully examining the small piece of dirt he had removed, before depositing it in his overflowing wastebasket.

"But you weren't in the least tempted to become better acquainted with her?" The policeman didn't look up, but his thin lips spread in a wide grin. "It seems to me you might have missed out on quite an opportunity, Merisi. Come on, now—let's quit kidding. I imagine most men would have wanted—probably tried their damnedest, in fact—to get to know her. A beautiful girl like that walking up to them, showing off everything she had. Yeah, and it sure as hell looked to me like she had plenty of goodies to show you, too. Even more interesting if she seemed . . . well, as you said, kinda kinky. Don't you agree?"

"No. I wasn't interested," said Mick. You bastard, he thought. Most men, maybe, but not me.

Shall I tell you why I wasn't interested, Jerry? You too, George. Shall I tell you about the Moroccan girl who shared my small table at Chez Madame Germaine one rainy night in Paris? God, she was lovely—café au lait skin with large Van Dyke brown almond eyes—had a most interesting indigo tattoo on her left ankle, too. She'd just been dumped by her French lover and was almost as lonely as I was. I tried that night—God, how I tried! But I couldn't manage it with her because, sweet and willing as she was, she just wasn't Claudia.

Or would you rather hear about the waitress in Santa Fe? She was a former student of mine, not much of a painter, but Jesus Christ, what a body! Still, not all her seemingly genuine pleasure in meeting me again—sexy whispers about how my work had always made her feel she really understood me—more than a few glasses of a pretty good Meursault (God, I can remember when just the bouquet of that wine used to turn me on!)—the smell of a crackling piñon fire in the white kiva fireplace with a tape of U2 playing on the stereo—none of those things could make me forget she wasn't Claudia, either. After my humiliating performance, or should I say lack of one that night, when I left her place, I also left New Mexico for good. Just started driving. It took me almost three months of sleeping in National Parks to decide I had to come back here, or die.

Hell, I can't paint. I can't make love to women. I don't even try anymore. But it was almost as if that damned girl on the beach knew it—was taunting me with it.

But as Mick thought all this he only said, "I wasn't interested. And it's no one's business why not. Besides, it looked as though she was spoken for that evening because I saw a man standing under the bluffs. It looked like he was waiting there for someone, and that someone sure as hell wasn't me."

Jerry picked up the girl's picture and tapped its thin edge on the desk. "She didn't tell you her name?"

"She didn't tell me anything."

"Or where she was staying?"

"No. As I said before, she didn't tell me anything at all."

Jerry got up and began to pace the small room. "Even by daylight it's no easy walk to that beach along the shore—too many slippery rocks and boulders. Do you think she came by the road?"

"I didn't see her there. But it's possible. Penelope—Mrs. Winslow—and I were inside having a drink earlier. Someone could have walked down the road without our knowing it, I suppose."

"How about your tenants? Couldn't she have been staying with one of them? I understand Miss Glass is an old friend of yours. I also know she often has house guests. Weirdos, too, most of them. Of course, being one of these arty guys yourself, you probably don't agree. One man's meat, as the saying goes."

Mick shrugged off the implication. "She's got a Russian émigré painter staying with her right now. In fact, I thought it could have been him I saw on the beach that night, after I met him this morning. But when I stopped off to say hello to Trudy this morning, she certainly didn't mention anyone else, any girl staying there. It seems unlikely. As I imagine you know, her house guests are usually male."

To Mick's surprise, the information that it might have been Evgeny Otkresta on the beach that night didn't seem to interest the policeman at all. He had even stopped writing and appeared not to be listening any longer to what Mick said. He sat down again and frowned as he read over the notes he'd already taken.

"How about your other tenant? Isn't the second building, the small one, also rented?"

"My studio? Yes, but I don't know anything about that tenant. He was over on the mainland when I saw the girl."

"How do you know?"

"Penelope—Mrs. Winslow told me. She manages the rentals on my property, you know."

Jerry began to write again. "She never told you his name?"

"Yes. Mr. Meer."

"Anyone besides yourself staying with Mrs. Winslow?"

"I came over on the ferry with her daughter Cassandra, who's home from college now. Mr. Winslow isn't there, of course. I assume you know they're divorced."

Jerry leaned back in the chair, puffed his cheeks out, then blew out his breath noisily, shaking his head in apparent disbelief about something. "Oh, sure. Everyone knows that. Boy, I tell you—it sure takes all kinds! I saw Winslow at a restaurant in Newport a while ago, out on the town with some bimbo—all lovey-dovey they were. And Jesus, Penelope Winslow's a damned nice piece of ass! I'm telling you, I sure as hell wouldn't go looking elsewhere if I had something like that back home to snuggle up with. Would you, Merisi?"

Mick decided not to dignify the question with an answer. Jerry swiveled around in his chair and stared morosely out the grimy window. Then he abruptly faced Mick again, once more speaking in his usual officious manner, jotting down still more notes. "So I understand there's no one else in that area except Tom and Angie Girtin and their granddaughter?"

"As far as I know; but, as I told you, I've only been back two days after being away from here four years. I'm the wrong person to ask about that."

Their conversation was interrupted at that moment by the roar of a motorcycle coming to a stop outside the firehouse. Detective Caron came in, carrying a black-and-white helmet with a police insignia on it, and greeted them. Mick couldn't help musing upon the incongruity of this mild, bland man whipping around the island on a noisy and powerful motorcycle the way the few bored adolescent boys who lived year round on the island no doubt yearned to do.

"Okay, we won't be needing you anymore, now, George," said Jerry.

George threw Mick a knowing wink as he left.

44

Detective Caron picked up the clipboard Jerry handed him. He read quickly, then put it back on the desk.

"Anything more you want me to ask him?" Jerry's tone to Caron was a mixture of deference and fury. Mick wondered what it was about the small, mild detective that seemed to set off such hostility.

"No, thanks. Let's try to get an ID," said Caron. He turned to Mick. "Thanks again for your cooperation, Mr. Merisi. It's been a great help. Let me see . . . " He picked up the clipboard and studied it again. "I just want to make sure we know where to reach you, should we need to again. It says here you'll be staying with a Mrs. Penelope Winslow. And I notice we have her phone number down here, too. Very good. Excellent."

"But I'll only be there for a couple of days. I was planning on leaving soon for France." Suddenly inspired, Mick saw the small village in the South where he'd once spent three blissful weeks in springtime, drawing and sketching alone among the sweetly mingled smells of pine and almond trees. That had been a long time ago, before he ever met Claudia. There was a little farmhouse pension with one large room over the barn, room enough to set up his easel. Yes, that's where he'd go. It would be the perfect place to be—beautiful, but with no memories, except of Cézanne. It was a place where he could paint again.

Caron picked up the girl's picture and glanced at it, then tossed it carelessly onto the clipboard. "France, mm? My wife and I have always wanted to go there. Well, just let us know before you leave the island, will you?" he said, somewhat too casually, Mick thought.

"But you don't see any reason why I can't be on my way soon, do you?" Mick asked. He wanted to get away from the island, quickly. He wondered how he and Claudia could have ever loved it so, for at that moment he loathed the place and never wanted to see it again.

And he sure didn't like the direction this thing was heading.

"I doubt it, but keep in touch all the same." Caron smiled

perfunctorily and shook Mick's hand as he showed him out the door.

Dazed, Mick stepped out of the fire station into the outside air. The wind had come up stronger. A large gray cloud swelled ominously over the harbor. Whitecaps covered the water, whose surface was now leaden, reflecting the dun sky, and the air had turned chilly. Funny how island weather always changed so abruptly. He had forgotten.

He looked across the harbor and noticed Sandy in a sleek black wet suit, her strong young back arched toward the whitecaps, as she skimmed across the water on her windsurfing board. She jumped from the board into shallow water, just before it hit shore. She waved to someone on the dock, while with her other hand she grabbed the mast and expertly secured the board.

The bright emerald light blinking on the jetty and Sandy's cerise and violet sail were the only vivid colors on the scene. They appeared garish and out of place in all the surrounding pastel and muted tones. But only think of what Marquet, the great gray Fauve, would have made of it!

As Mick observed the scene, he shivered with no shirt to cover his bare chest. He began to walk fast to warm himself. Strange how hot it had been earlier that day, when flies had buzzed around the dead girl and he'd had to refresh her stiff body with cold seawater. Could he possibly have been in Jerry's office that long? Where was the girl now? he wondered. Some icy morgue, off there on the mainland. Mick shivered again.

As he trudged up the road he thought of all the things Jerry *hadn't* asked him, such as how he'd spent his morning before finding her, and what sort of camera the girl had used to take his picture. Surely there weren't that many young women around with the most expensive camera in the world to play with.

It bothered Mick also that Caron hadn't found more to say. It looked as though he would be staying on the island for the time being, not merely trusting things to Jerry, but watching and listening, and thinking for himself. Mick was sure the girl's camera would eventually be found. He decided it was a good thing he'd already told Jerry about her taking his picture before the police found it out for themselves.

Maybe he'd better call Chap Winslow that night, he thought. Get some legal advice from him. Chap was the only attorney he knew.

Once again Mick wished he'd never come back to Dutchman's Island. What had he expected it to prove anyway?

And now this.

When he reached the cottage, Penelope was kneeling in the garden, pulling weeds. The gathering clouds and the chill pale light surrounding her made her look, at that moment, like a figure in some small and tender scene by Chardin—so peaceful, so serene. For one brief moment Mick saw again the island as it had once looked to him; but as quickly as it had come, the vision vanished.

He didn't have the strength left in him to discuss the events of the day. He hoped to sneak past Penelope without being noticed, but Crosby came prancing out from among the young lettuces with a loud *miaow*. She leaped across the split oak basket lying full of chunks of wet earth and tangled, wilting weeds—ran to Mick and rubbed against his leg, purring her usual loud and loving greeting.

Penelope came over to him. "Mick?" she said, frowning. She removed a muddy gardening glove and gently touched his arm. "Mick, are you okay? No, you're not, are you? What's wrong?"

"Nothing, Penelope. No, that's not true—I'll explain. First let me go put a shirt on."

"Yes, you look cold. Would you like some tea, coffee, something to eat? Or maybe a drink?"

"I don't know if the sun's over the yardarm yet, but as long as you're offering it, I sure could use a drink."

As he climbed the steps to the guest quarters over the garage, he heard the Subaru pull into the driveway. Sandy didn't notice him as she jumped out and darted toward Penelope.

"Mom! Did you hear what happened? It looks like Mr. Girtin finally went and did it—just like Dad always said he would!"

"Did what?" Penelope bent down absently to pat Crosby, who

was following her inside. "Listen, sweetheart, you'd better hurry and get into some dry clothes. Your teeth are chattering."

"I will, Mom, in a minute. But first let me tell you what happened today. They said Mr. Girtin shot some girl he found snooping around in the dunes. Everybody down at the harbor is talking about it. Nobody knows who she was, but I overheard someone say she's dead!"

CHAPTER

Six

" . . . WITH A HASSELBLAD."

Sandy stared at Mick, then drew in her breath with a quick gasp. "Are you sure it was a Hasselblad?"

"Yes. Why? Do you know what that is—a very expensive Swedish camera? Quite an unusual piece of equipment for a kid her age to have."

Sandy continued to stare, hesitating before speaking again. "Mr. Merisi, that painting you mentioned—the one you said she looked like—that's the girl standing nude on the scallop shell with flowers floating in the air around her, right?"

"That's the one. You probably had it in Art History 101. Almost everyone does."

"Yes, we did—all of us, I mean." Sandy suddenly sprang from her chair, knocking it over. Mick thought she looked pale. "Mom, I forgot—I told Johnny I'd meet him. I'd better go."

"Will you be back for dinner?" Penelope called after her, but the back door had already slammed and the Subaru started up.

Mick and Penelope sat in awkward silence until finally she said, "I'm so sorry it had to be you who found that poor girl today,

Mick. What a terrible thing for anyone to see, but you of all people . . . "

He drank down the last of his Scotch. For a moment he thought he would tell Penelope he'd thought the dead girl might really be Claudia at last—both the night he first saw her rising from the waves and then again, today, when he'd discovered her body lying on the beach. He felt she would be sympathetic. After all, she too had loved Claudia. Yes, maybe Penelope was the only person in the world who might understand what he felt.

But he didn't. He decided there was no point in letting anyone see how desperate, how crazy he was becoming. Because it *was* crazy to go on searching everywhere for someone who'd been dead four years, he knew that. Yet here on Dutchman's Island the visits, the voices, the hallucinations were becoming more frequent. Mick wondered if he shouldn't try to contact that doctor he'd seen on late night TV at that dreary motel in Tucson—the psychiatrist out in California who specialized in grief therapy . . .

Oh hell! What did he know? What did anyone know? Even Penelope.

"Mick?" She spoke softly.

"What? I'm sorry—what were you saying?"

"I was just wondering if you wanted another drink?"

He looked at the empty glass in his hand and shook his head. "No, thanks. Listen, I've got an idea. How about going down to Vinnie's for supper? It might get our minds off all this. Besides," he forced a smile, "you've been doing too much cooking for me lately. It's my turn to feed you for a change." Mick suddenly felt a need to be surrounded by the pointless din of strangers talking, eating, drinking, laughing.

"That's a great idea." She stood up. "Let me take a minute to get out of my gardening clothes and leave Sandy a note."

As soon as they had climbed the weatherbeaten outside stairs to the Clam Bar and opened the door, Mick saw that here, too, nothing had changed since he'd been gone. There were the same tables gleaming with many glassy coats of spar varnish, each place set with a scallop-edged paper placemat decorated with a spindly drawing of a Maine lobster. Miniature hurricane lamps substituted for candlelight. Lengths of fishnet were draped over the windows, dangling their cork bobbers and blue glass balls. A pair of oars was fastened to the pine-paneled wall, which was itself covered with the names of many pairs of lovers enclosed in crudely drawn hearts pierced by Cupid's arrows. Vinnie still presided, large and smiling, over the long bar. An old but still glittering green cardboard shamrock hung drunkenly over the mirror behind the cash register, a remnant of some festive St. Patrick's Day long past.

They hung their rain gear in the alcove just inside the top of the stairs. As soon as they stepped through the door, Mick whispered, "Oh Jesus, Penelope. Look who's here!"

Jerry Francis sat alone at the bar. He wore off-duty clothes, a Hawaiian shirt hanging out over the waist of a pair of baggy red Breton sailing pants. He was staring gloomily into a double straight-up martini—one of Vinnie's specialties.

Except for him, the place was empty of customers. Mick hoped he and Penelope could make a quick exit, but before he had a chance to whisper this to her, she said, "Good evening, Vinnie, Jerry."

"Evening, Penelope," boomed Vinnie. "Hey! What do you know! Will you just take a look at what the cat dragged in?"

Jerry slid down from the bar stool and walked out the door without finishing his drink.

"So long, Jerry." Vinnie gave a quick wave to him. "Take care."

He turned to Mick, clasped both his hands, and pumped them vigorously. "Mick Merisi! I'll be a son of a gun! Boy, it's good to see you again—I can't tell you how good!"

He motioned to a table overlooking the harbor. As soon as he brought drinks, he said, "You folks hear they found a body down at Wrecker's Point?"

"Mick was the one who found her," Penelope said solemnly.

"Oh Jeez—sorry! I didn't know that. What happened, anyway? Old Tommy get crazy with his shotgun? That's what I heard. I tried to weasel some more information out of Jerry, but he's not talking."

"I don't think it was a gun, Vinnie," said Mick. "There wasn't any blood."

Vinnie whistled. "No wonder Jerry's so shook up."

Mick raised his eyebrows quizzically.

"I mean," Vinnie went on, "here he's been waiting for a real crime to solve for years—you know he used to be a detective, don't you?"

"No, I never heard that," Mick said. "Did you?" He turned to Penelope.

"I think I did," she replied.

"Anyway," Vinnie resumed his story, "when he finally gets his big chance, along comes some cop from the mainland to take the case away from him. This guy even told him to take the night off. Can you believe it? Old Jerry was in real bad shape before you two got here, mad as hell." He pulled a menu from his apron pocket. "So what can I get you for dinner? Fluke's nice and fresh."

As Mick and Penelope ate the sweet, icy littlenecks they'd ordered for a first course, she was silent. Mick watched darkness creep over the harbor. The only light was a glowing window upstairs at Palmer's Boatyard. He could hear the mournful sound of the bell buoy until Vinnie turned on the jukebox and the unmistakable voice of Frank Sinatra came on, singing some song Mick had never heard before. Vinnie, however, seemed to know it well, for he sang along loudly and tunelessly.

Penelope speared a raw, pink clam, dipped it in blood red sauce, then ate it daintily.

It was Claudia who had first introduced Mick to clams on the half shell. As he watched Penelope eat hers as gracefully and skillfully as Claudia would have, he began to suspect that, unlike himself, natives of coastal New England were simply born knowing how to do it. Mick had always been somewhat troubled by the thought that the clams on his plate, delicious as they tasted, were still alive, or nearly so.

He wasn't at all surprised to see Detective Caron enter the room just as Vinnie brought sizzling plates of grilled fish from the kitchen. Caron acknowledged Mick's presence with a curt nod, then turned to the bar and waited for Vinnie. He spoke briefly, and although his back was to Mick, he was quite sure the detective showed Vinnie the Polaroids that had been taken that afternoon. Caron spoke softly and Mick couldn't hear what he said.

Vinnie came over to their table and said, "Listen, folks, I'm just going to step out in the hall with this gentleman for a minute. You all set for now?"

"Sure," said Mick. He filled Penelope's glass with chilled white wine. "That's the detective I told you about. I think he was showing pictures of the girl to Vinnie. I wonder if he knew her?"

"I don't think she's from the island, Mick—not from your description, anyway." She took her paper napkin and discreetly wiped her mouth. Mick was unable to equate her ladylike, even somewhat prim manner with Jerry's earlier crude remarks about her.

"Penelope, how well do you know Jerry Francis?"

"Not well at all, and I don't care to, either, thank you." Even in the dim lamplight Mick could tell she was blushing. "Why? Did he say anything about me to you?"

"Nothing worth repeating."

She began nervously tearing the edges of her napkin into fringe. "After Chap and I were divorced, he started dropping in on me at the house sometimes. At first, I'd offer him a cup of tea while he told me his life story. Now I wish I hadn't."

"Why?"

"Because I loathe him. I was just being polite, and I shouldn't have been."

"It encouraged him, you mean?"

"I suppose. But that certainly wasn't my intent. He's had an unhappy time of it, I'll admit that, but I think he probably brought it all on himself. It seems he handled some investigation improperly a few years ago. He was subsequently removed from his position and given a job out here on the island—you know—

handing out enormous parking fines to summer visitors to save the islanders from paying larger property taxes."

Mick smiled. No, Dutchman's Island hadn't changed. Sandy was right.

"Oh, yes," Penelope continued, "and his wife divorced him at about the same time. He didn't tell me why, but I'm sure she had good reasons. But you know, Mick, he never felt this great need to tell me his tale of woe while Chap and I were still married . . . "

"So now that you're on your own, he thinks he's entitled to some sort of claim on you? *Droit de seigneur,* or something like that?" As soon as he had said it, Mick wished he hadn't.

But she didn't appear offended, only nodded gravely in apparent agreement. "I finally told him I didn't like people dropping in on me without telephoning first. So now he telephones often—too often—to invite me to dinner. He looked angry when he saw me come in here with you, didn't he?"

"Could be. He doesn't like me."

"I always say no to him, but he absolutely never gives up. One day I'm going run out of excuses." She spoke softly but intensely. "I hate him."

Vinnie came back alone. Mick excused himself and walked over to the bar. "What do you think, Vinnie? Did you know her?"

"Not by name. But she'd been in here, Monday night. Quite a scene that was, too."

"Why? What happened?"

"Well, she was meeting up with that foreign guy who's staying with Miss Glass. You know him?"

So it *must* have been Evgeny waiting for her on the beach that night . . .

"I've met him."

"Nervous guy," Vinnie continued. "I noticed his hands shaking—that is, until he got a shot of vodka down. What is he, Polish or something?"

"Russian, I think."

"Figures. I've heard they really like their vodka. Anyway, before you know it, Miss Glass came in and gave it to the girl. You couldn't hear a word she said, but you could tell she was damned mad. Then the guy started shouting, but I couldn't understand him."

"What about the girl?"

Vinnie hesitated. "I don't know if I should be telling you all this stuff. . . . " He sighed. "Oh, what the hell."

"I appreciate it, Vinnie. Jerry gave me a rough time of it this afternoon. I'm relieved to hear you'd seen her, because I had, too. Tuesday night on the beach in front of my studio—the night I got here."

"No kidding? Then you must know what I mean about her. Boy, wasn't she something?"

"Good-looking, you mean?"

"Yeah, that—but that's not all. She was so icy cool. Just as cool as she could be. Even when Miss Glass slapped her face, she didn't slap back; just stood there smiling with that big red smack mark across her cheek."

Mick could see once more the girl's mocking expression as she took his picture. "What happened after that?"

"They left—Miss Glass and the guy, I mean."

"Without her?"

"Yeah. As I said, she was a real cool one. Classy, too, nothing like most kids her age. I don't know—maybe she was older than she looked. God, she sure was some beautiful girl. Poor kid." He stopped talking and filled a bowl with peanuts.

Mick asked for another Scotch.

As soon as Vinnie had poured it, the bartender resumed his story without further urging. "Anyway, she came over and sat down at the bar, just as though nothing had happened. She ordered a Diet Coke and then asked me if I knew where she could get some sailing lessons. Can you believe it?"

Mick shook his head, acknowledging Vinnie's question.

"I told her I'd heard Johnny Selcott was planning on running a windsurfing school this summer—that was the only kind of sailing lesson I knew of. She thanked me and said she'd look into it." He pointed to Mick's glass. "Another?"

"No, thanks. That's it for me. Was that all you talked about?"

"No. She also wanted to know how she'd go about renting a small house or apartment for the season, and I said she'd have to get in touch with that pretty lady over there." He pointed to Penelope. "Anyway, then she finished her Coke and left."

Vinnie's reference to Penelope abruptly reminded Mick how rude he'd been to leave her sitting alone at the table.

"Excuse me," he said as he left the bar and returned to her. "God—I'm sorry I didn't come back before this, Penelope. Come on over to the bar with me. Vinnie's just given me some very interesting information. Apparently the girl was a friend of Trudy's boy toy."

"Really? The Russian one? I never saw him with anyone. Still . . . " Penelope frowned, then closed her eyes and shuddered. Mick wondered if she was afraid that if she looked around, she, too, might see the dead girl's body.

"Jeez!" Vinnie exclaimed as soon as they came back to the bar. "I tell you, whoever did that is some monster. You know, I don't think there's ever been a murder on the island. At least, not one anybody can remember." He picked up the bottle of whiskey. "How about it, Mick? Want a refill?"

"No, thanks." Mick put his hand over his empty glass. "Listen, Vinnie—she never said where she was staying, or gave you her name?"

"Nope. You know, I never thought to card her. She looked young, but somehow, I didn't care. That's the only way I ever pick up a name from the young folks." He began to mop up the counter with a dish towel. "Hey, you never told me, how was dinner?"

"It was terrific, Vinnie, as always."

He and Penelope left without coffee or dessert. It had begun to rain—a cold drizzle that wouldn't let up soon. Mick started up the van and swung around in the opposite direction from Penelope's house.

"Where are we going?" she asked.

"I just thought I'd like to see the rest of the island. You don't mind going home the long way around, do you?"

She shook her head. "Not at all."

On the dark road that wound about the small island, Mick hit the brakes hard as a deer jumped out of the high bayberry bushes, easily clearing a stone wall and the width of the blacktop road. It leaped quickly—only a flash of white and gold in the glaring headlights.

They passed the old unused lighthouse that loomed up off the road, massive, gray, and ghostly. "I remember when we used to all go there on picnics sometimes," Penelope said. "Do you remember, Mick? Playing volleyball—you and Chap against me and Sandy and Claudia?"

"I remember. Your team always won."

They were both silent as he continued around the island. When the road dipped and rounded the westernmost end of it, he saw a spotlight scanning first the starless sky, then the beach and sea. Finally the powerful streak of light flashed up into the dunes before beginning its roving search again.

"Looks like the police are still at it, rain or no rain," Mick commented.

"I hope they find whoever did it soon." Penelope gazed out the window at the light. "She was about Sandy's age, wasn't she, Mick?"

"I think so."

He turned into the dirt road by her house and was glad to see the Subaru already parked in the driveway ahead of him.

C H A P T E R

Seven

THE SEA WAS flat and shining, a slick tar black, without waves. Mick gazed at it from the rear window of his room. He couldn't sleep, even though the rain had finally let up and the spotlights had given up their search for the night.

The clouds that hid the silver moon scuttled away, as in one of those dark seascapes born of Ryder's mystical dreaming. In that brief moment Mick was sure he saw someone—the dark shadow of some unknown person walking slowly up the road toward the Winslow house. Soon clouds again covered the moon, and whoever it was disappeared from sight. Yet even though the figure he had seen walked slowly, Mick thought he could hear someone else's footsteps running along the dirt road.

He looked out the front window that faced the house. He saw no one. All was quiet. The kitchen light went out—the only visible sign of life now settling down for the night. He lay down on his bed and stared at the sky as he fell into a long and dreamless sleep.

When he awoke, his shades were still up. It seemed late in the morning, for the sun was high. He watched a brilliant slash of scarlet fluttering in the clear blue sky. He could hear a ripping, tearing sound and soon realized the same red kite he had seen the day before was flying again, the fresh wind from the sea pulling and pushing eagerly at its gleaming mylar surface.

Mick sat up to obtain a better view out the window. He was surprised to see Evgeny Otkresta standing alone on the high lawn of the cottage, carefully unreeling the twine that held the kite. He followed the soaring line almost to the road. Mick noticed the Russian was smiling as he looked up at the kite, a jubilant and boyish smile.

The kite fluttered, shimmied, and took a sudden dive. It fell into the impenetrable bayberry thicket, its lifeline tangled in branches.

Evgeny crossed the road. He tried to reach the branches where the kite lay, but quickly realized the dense bushes made this impossible. Then he angrily pulled a knife from his pocket and cut the twine. When he walked back toward the cottage, there was a depressed and weary stoop to his back.

Mick showered and changed his clothes. He noticed Penelope's car was gone, but an old Jeep was parked next to Sandy's Subaru. Day-Glo bumper stickers advertising the manufacturers of various sailboards were stuck on bumpers, windows, doors, making Mick assume it belonged to Johnny Selcott. An image of a sunburnt, towheaded adolescent boy pumping gas down at Selcott's Mobil Station came to him. But of course he was grown-up now, like Sandy. Murmurs from the girl's open window convinced him the two of them were taking advantage of her mother's absence to be alone.

Mick got in the van and drove up to the airport, remembering they used to sell coffee and doughnuts there.

No one was inside the small and flimsy building that was the waiting room for the airport. A pilot Mick didn't recognize stood on the grass runway putting a Louis Vuitton briefcase into the small prop plane. When he went around to the other side and climbed into his seat, Mick saw that one of his two passengers was Trudy Glass.

He drank bitter, black coffee from a Styrofoam cup and ate a stale and greasy doughnut while he watched the plane fly over the water. Mick hadn't appreciated Penelope's coffee until then. But any food or drink seemed to calm the anxiety he felt in his throat and chest on seeing the plane take off.

One more hurdle leaped.

He was surprised to see Trudy leaving the island today—after the story Vinnie had told him. He wondered why she and her young Russian friend weren't being interrogated by the police, as he had been. He picked up a newspaper, wondering if there was any news about the girl's death. He didn't stay to read it, but took it with him and drove off.

As he drove slowly around the island, it struck him that the whole place seemed to have taken on a peculiar, deep silence that morning. Nothing seemed connected to anything else. It was as though the girl's ghost had cast a spell over all the surroundings. He remembered a similar doomed silence the day after Claudia's plane went down.

Mick passed no other car. It seemed as if his steering wheel now turned of its own accord, taking him wherever the van itself decided to go. There was only one paved road around the island, but there were numerous dirt roads. Some of them had names crudely painted on granite rocks standing at their entrance, while others had names known only in island lore passed on from father to son. The dirt roads were sometimes represented by thin lines on Coast Guard sounding charts, for the island had been a place of mine and submarine activity during World War II. But more often they were not, and they were never indicated on the carelessly drawn decorative maps given out to visitors at the ferry dock and airport. These secret roads were usually assumed by visitors to be driveways, probably leading to houses hidden by dense vegetation. Islanders preferred it that way, for the natives of Dutchman's Island had a long and well-founded mistrust of strangers.

The original seventeenth-century settlers had watched from the island for ships at sea—ships that could be lured by fires they set on the beaches onto treacherous and dangerous rocks lying just offshore. When the vessels crashed onto these rocks, their valuable cargo was plundered while passengers and crew were left to drown. The oldest families on the island still bore the names of those infamous wreckers: Chapman, Palmer, Selcott, Potter, Bigelow, Winslow.

The van turned left onto a dirt road that led toward the uninhabited center of the island, crossing the wreckers' highest lookout hill. Soon the road narrowed as it headed downhill. Now Mick understood where he was going, where he was being drawn by Claudia. It wasn't long before he pulled the van off the road, dumped the rest of his coffee on the weeds, and got out, still carrying the cup.

There was a barely discernible path leading through a blackberry bramble. He and Claudia used to come here late in summer to gather ripe blackberries whose small, swollen, purple globules hung clustered together.

"No one else ever comes here for berries. Just us," Claudia would say, as she fed him the biggest and sweetest one she'd picked, staining his lips with deep purple which she soon kissed away.

It was always quiet there, except for the drone of honeybees who came to suck from the last white berry blossoms. Bees were buzzing loudly that morning. The thorny bramble bushes were covered with flowers and the insects' tiny legs were yellow and heavy with powdery pollen.

Mick walked along the path until he heard the sound of water gushing. The island was filled with secret springs of fresh water. This one tumbled out of and over a large pink granite rock. Green moss grew around the spouting stream. When Mick reached it, he filled his cup and drank. It was icy cold, tasting of stone and silence. Drinking it, even from the Styrofoam cup, Mick had always felt he was partaking of holy elixir. It had always been like that when he drank this water. The place was a sort of Arcadia where he expected to see Poussin's noble nymphs and gods come dancing through it.

He filled his cup again and drank, then waited for her to speak to him.

"This way, Mick." Her voice was soft, enticing.

He walked further along the path until it was almost gone. Then he came to a place where a grove of cool, fragrant pine surrounded him.

He made his way through the low-lying pine branches, stooping as he walked. The ground glowed red with years of shining needles. He could see those palpable lavender shadows Mick had always believed Cézanne invented. That is—until he first stood in this place.

The sun shone brightly beyond the pine grove. There was a fresh water pond there, a pond born of endlessly flowing deep springs. Water lilies raised their waxy petals to the cloudless sky. Mick pulled off his shoes and stepped into the water.

In every one of the many visits he had made with Claudia to this place, they had never seen another person. But today someone else sat in the shade of the pines, staring silently at the water. Whoever it was rose quickly and disappeared among the trees, avoiding him.

Mick followed. A man was standing perfectly still, his back to Mick.

"Sam?" Mick said, suddenly recognizing Sam Palmer.

He turned around quickly. "Hello, Mick. What are you doing here?"

Mick didn't know himself, at that point. This was one more place he had to say a final farewell to—that was all.

It was obvious Sam hadn't expected to meet anyone else there, either. When he spoke again it was in a quiet voice, so quiet Mick could hardly hear him—almost as though he was talking to himself. "Claudia must have brought you here."

Don't be smug, Mick wanted suddenly to say. Don't rub it in that my wife, my only love, was once your girl.

Claudia had spent the summer she was sixteen going steady with Sam Palmer. It was a part of her life Mick resented. She'd made it sound like a childish, romantic, but chaste interlude. But it was also the year she'd learned to sail—the year Aunt Betsy had given her *Felicity* for her birthday. Sam had taught her how to fill the sail with wind and go cutting through the waves. It was a summer she'd spent working at the boatyard, helping him restore the wreck that was *Luna* then to its former glory. Mick suspected it was also an interlude that meant far more to Claudia than she would admit, for she would never talk about Sam with him. What little he knew of it came from a few inadvertent and tactless remarks Chap Winslow had occasionally made. Mick was admittedly jealous of this secret part of her, this part he couldn't reach.

Suddenly he hated the place, knowing she'd been there with someone else before him. He had wanted to believe it was their place—theirs alone. Now the illusion was lost forever. But something made him stay, to ask questions whose answers he didn't really want to hear.

"Did you come here often with her?"

"Yes, I did," Sam replied. "My grandfather owned this land, you know. The big hill, the pond—all of it." He gestured widely with his arm. "My father inherited it, but we never lived on it, never worked the land the way the others had. I always thought that was a shame, somehow."

She had never told Mick that. "So you own it, now?"

Sam nodded. "Ninety-three acres. The old house and barn came down in a hurricane about ten years ago." He paused, seeming deep in thought. "No point in building them up again," he said, as though he'd just decided that.

Mick didn't want to hear any more. Why hadn't Claudia ever told him this property belonged to Sam Palmer? Strange that she hadn't.

The two of them stood silently staring at the water lilies. Blue and red dragonflies with tails like bolts of neon landed on the lily pads. "She thought this was the most beautiful place on earth," Sam said, as he skipped a stone expertly across the still surface of the pond. The dragonflies darted away. "But I'm sure you know that. She must have told you."

Mick said nothing.

"She was a wonderful person," Sam added. "I think about her

often. I know"—he picked up another pebble and skipped it across the pond—"I know how great your loss was, Mick. I'm sorry I've never known how to say that to you before."

Mick nodded. He tried to recall Sam's wife. Sarah Palmer wore a crabbed and pinched look of perpetual disappointment as she sat in the post office day after day, where she had the lifetime job of postmistress. Here she doled out stamps for small change, scornfully examined packages wrapped in wrinkled brown paper and secondhand string, made old women with stiffened arthritic fingers rewrite the penciled addresses on their letters to faraway offspring. Sarah and Sam had no children, and Mick wondered what kept them together, for they had always struck him as a singularly mismatched couple. Sarah represented the mean and grasping side of the islanders—it was easy to imagine *her* ancestors as wreckers. Sam, on the other hand, had a laconic Yankee serenity that Mick believed came from his long and loving relationship with the sea, for Claudia had always had it, too.

He felt pity for Sam Palmer; after all, it had been himself—Mick Merisi—who Claudia had loved and married. Who she chose to be with forever. For the first time Mick understood that Sam's distant, even unfriendly manner, which he had been sure resulted from jealousy, hid some deep and unspeakable sadness.

Sam had become uncharacteristically talkative. "She always knew she was welcome here, you know. Always—didn't ever have to ask. You know, I never did bother to put up any of those 'No Trespassing' signs because no one ever came here but her. And me," he added, moving off and brushing pine needles from his jeans.

What about me? Mick wished he had included him with Claudia, although Sam was obviously referring to another time—his own time with her, long ago. But it was me she loved at the end. Mick wanted to say it aloud, shout it, but the words didn't come.

They walked out of the grove together. "I'm curious as to how you got here," Mick said, trying to end their meeting in a friendly but casual manner. "I didn't see your truck anywhere."

"There's another path, over this way." Sam pointed in the opposite direction. "I'm parked off Hawk Run."

"I never knew Hawk Run led up here." There must be so many more secret walkways on the island Claudia hadn't revealed to him. But Mick had always thought he knew them all, the way Sam did.

"No," replied Sam. "I don't expect you did."

He had that New England way of turning aloof and cool, just when you were beginning to feel at ease with him. Penelope had it, too, Mick had noticed lately.

He was about to ask Sam if he'd heard about the girl's death at Wrecker's Point, but Sam seemed to want to end their conversation when he said, "Will you be around long?"

"No, I'm planning on leaving the island soon, for good."

Sam said nothing. Instead, he reached down and picked up a small piece of orange cardboard he'd spotted lying on the ground, then stuffed it in his pocket. "Some folks sure don't know how to treat a place like this—leaving their filthy garbage all over." His lips curled in disgust.

"You might have to put up some of those 'No Trespassing' signs after all, Sam. Lots of people—summer people, tourists—they're starting to discover Dutchman's Island."

"Yeah, too many of them, that's for damned sure." Sam looked at Mick with an expression that reminded him he too was merely one of those people—an off-islander, an outsider, an enemy.

He turned and walked away without saying anything more.

Eight

THE WEEKEND CAME and went, but nothing happened.

Then on Monday, Detective Caron knocked on the door of Mick's room. With him was another detective named Reynolds, a young black man. Jerry wasn't there.

"What's happening, Mick? What do they want?" Penelope asked.

"Nothing much. They just want to go over a few of the things I told Jerry. Double-checking, I guess. I'll tell you about it later."

The air was fresh and sparkling. The island's ubiquitous wild roses were in full bloom now, tumbling and sprawling around the foundation of the silver-shingled garage. The curling tendrils of sweet peas wound around the thorny rose canes, their vulvalike flowers tempting butterflies down from the sky. For a brief moment Mick felt regret that he would be leaving the island, as soon after his interview was over as was possible. When he had filled in some small detail Jerry had neglected to ask him about—probably when he gave them a little more information about the man he saw on the beach that night—then his unwilling connection with the dead girl would be broken. He would be free to leave.

His visit had accomplished nothing, for he would never be free of Claudia. He had been a fool to try.

As Mick turned out onto the paved road, he caught a glimpse of the scarlet kite lying still and lifeless on the vast expanse of bayberry moor. A long gash had ripped through its shining surface, allowing a dead, leafless branch to poke through, securing it to the bushes. There were a few bird droppings, chalky white specks on red.

The questions Caron and Reynolds asked were brief. Mick felt he'd been right in assuming they only wanted to confirm things he'd already told Jerry, although what the point of the questions was he still failed to see.

When he was finished, Mick aimlessly drove around the island and finally parked the van out by the highest bluffs, the ones facing the open Atlantic. He sat on the edge of the bluff for a long time, watching the long ocean waves roll majestically in to shore, and wondering if you sailed straight out, would the next land you saw be Spain, Portugal, or France?

A couple of college kids walked past him, carrying a large canvas tote bag and a sun-faded quilt. They climbed down the rickety stairs to the shore, the girl giggling as the boy whispered in her ear. Was it like that once with Claudia and Sam Palmer? he wondered. Why hadn't she ever told him she used to go to the water-lily pond with Sam—told him that Sam owned the land she had led him to believe was theirs alone? He felt betrayed, angry at her, for he suspected—not for the first time—that Claudia's teenage romance with Palmer had meant much more to her than she'd indicated, that it went on meaning something, even after Mick, for she never spoke of it with him.

Oh hell, he decided, impatient with the direction his thoughts were wandering, it was just discretion and concern for my feelings. Christ, I wouldn't have talked with her about girls I'd spent my summers doing that with . . . Mick looked away from the sea, for the college girl and her boyfriend had wasted no time before starting to make love on the quilt.

He got up, marveling at the lack of any need for preliminary lovemaking kids had, and drove back to Penelope's place. No one was home, so he took the occasion to clean out the van for the first time in months, even borrowing a vacuum cleaner from the cleaning cupboard in the mud room to get rid of the cat hairs. "Damned cat," he muttered. "What the hell am I going to do with her when I leave?"

Around five o'clock Mick realized he'd forgotten to eat lunch, as he often did. He remembered Penelope mentioning she was planning on going over to the mainland that afternoon and Sandy was nowhere in sight. Since neither would be there for dinner, he decided to eat alone at Vinnie's.

He was glad to see the place jumping with a large crowd of sport fishermen, noisy and boastful from the salt air and sun, the glory of the chase, male companionship of the sort Mick didn't particularly enjoy—helped along by plenty of booze.

Vinnie appeared harassed from waiting on the large group alone, unable to gossip with him. Mick was glad the bartender couldn't talk about the dead girl with him. He felt safe—now that the matter was in the hands of two competent professionals like Caron and Reynolds, not left to the judgment of a lunatic like Jerry. There was nothing more he needed or wanted to know about the girl he'd found on the beach at Wrecker's Point.

He left the Clam Bar just as the sun was starting to set. When he arrived at the house he saw Penelope sitting on the porch swing in the fading light, bent over a piece of needlepoint. Her hair was cut short and formed small golden ringlets around her face, like the hair on some Fra Angelico angel.

"Hey," he said, "I hardly recognized you. You look great, like a little kid."

She smiled and ran her fingers through the curls. "Thanks. It feels wonderful. Don't you remember how I always got it chopped off like this as soon as the water got warm enough for swimming?"

"I don't know, maybe . . . " But he didn't.

"No," she said, "of course you don't remember. It's been such

68

a long time. Anyway, tell me—how did it go, the interview this afternoon?"

"It was okay." Mick's conversation with the two detectives now seemed to belong to the distant past. He had a wonderful feeling of peace and relief that it was all over. "They asked a lot of ridiculous questions, such as did anyone ever come to fish off the beach in front of the studio—that kind of thing. All of it seemed pointless, frankly. I don't know what they were trying to find out, but my answers seemed to satisfy them, because all of a sudden"—he snapped his fingers—"just like that, the interview was over. Anyway, I imagine they're finished with me now, thank God. I guess I can leave the island."

"And will you? I thought you were planning to stay for awhile." Crosby jumped onto Penelope's lap, kneading the needlepoint with gentle paws.

"I was—but I've changed my mind. I think I should go. It wasn't a good idea to come back here, Penelope, not a good idea at all." He sighed. "Too damned many memories."

She said nothing, just seemed to wait for him to continue.

"I'm thinking I'd like to go to France. I was happy living alone there once. I'll get a fresh start and get back to work. I'm ready to. Finally . . . " For a moment Mick could feel a brush in his hand, then the sensuous buttery flow of oil paint onto a freshly primed and stretched linen canvas. An image began to form in his mind, but quickly vanished.

Penelope nodded solemnly. "I did happen to speak with Ian Meer today about finding another place for him to stay for the summer so you could move back into your studio. I've got a couple of possibilities in mind. He said he'd think about it and let me know in a day or two. But I guess it doesn't matter now, does it?"

"No. Thanks, anyway. But I'd certainly appreciate it if I could spend a couple more days here with you. Just until I get a plane ticket and get myself organized enough to leave." He looked at her. "Will that be okay?"

"Of course. You know you're always welcome here any time, for as long as you wish." She stood up abruptly, letting both her needlepoint and Crosby fall to the floor. "Listen, Mick, how would you like to help me stake my tomato plants before it gets too dark? I almost forgot about them—the poor things are creeping along the ground. Sandy said she'd give me a hand, but she's not home yet. She must have already started to work at Vinnie's. I forgot when she said she would . . . "

Mick followed her into the backyard. "I didn't see her when I ate there tonight."

"Oh, she was probably in the kitchen, or—who knows? Perhaps she's off somewhere with Johnny. Here, just hold the vine to the stake like this, while I tie it."

Penelope stood back and studied the tomato vine, frowning slightly and biting her lower lip in profound concentration. She finally decided she approved of the way it was positioned on the stake, and she and Mick continued to work silently together until it grew dark. The peppery smell of green growing tomatoes filled the night air. Fireflies blinked and crickets chirped while giant dusty-winged moths bounced against the window screens, yearning for the lamplight inside. Far off across the water, lights on the mainland twinkled and there was everywhere the sound of ocean waves breaking endlessly on the island's shores.

Crosby rubbed against Penelope's legs, purring loudly. "You know, I'm really going to miss her," she said. "And you, too, of course."

Mick picked up the cat and handed her to Penelope. "How about letting Crosby stay here on the island with you for a while? She seems to adore you. God, Penelope—I'd appreciate it so. The way I always appreciate everything you do for me," he added.

"You're right. It will be much easier on her not to have all that plane travel, especially since you'll be coming back before long." She rubbed noses with Crosby. "She'll be good company for me, since I hardly ever see my daughter these days. Crosby's such a sweet little cat."

For a moment her gesture reminded Mick of Claudia.

He felt guilty. One way or another, he realized, he was always imposing on Penelope, and one way or another, she was always a good sport about it. He decided not to mention his plans to sell, not right now. He'd let the leases on the two houses run for the rest of the summer. Then, when he was settled in France, he'd write Penelope and tell her to put the property on the market— all of it. But not tonight. Only two nights ago at supper she'd been talking heatedly about the ever-growing number of real estate speculators who were coming after her these days looking for land to buy. She hated to see any big parcel of land come up for sale, only to be turned into hastily thrown-together cottages or condominiums that destroyed forever the island's ancient stone walls and bayberry moors. For Penelope, although not an islander herself, loved it the way Claudia had.

"Mick," she said. "Did the police ever tell you who she was?"

"The girl? No, and I didn't ask. For some reason I don't want to know. Does that make any sense to you?"

"The poor kid," was her only reply.

"Listen, isn't that your phone?" Mick was glad to change the subject.

"Was it? I didn't hear it ringing." She glanced toward the kitchen window. "Anyway, it's stopped now. The answering machine should have picked up, but Sandy probably forgot to turn it on when she went out. If it's important, I'm sure whoever it was will call back. It's probably for her, anyway."

She picked up a faded denim drawstring bag from the ground, filled with an ancient and motley collection of torn rags she'd used to tie the tomatoes. The vines looked somehow pathetic now, Mick thought, with their wild and prickly sprawling confined by the torn, frayed ghosts of white sheets that drooped in the darkness.

When they finished, the two of them returned to the porch and sat quietly listening to the night noises. An owl flew over the road, until its silent wings embraced the darkness shrouding the bayberry thicket. Mick heard some small beast's high-pitched final shriek.

Penelope stroked Crosby's spine. "Look how she's trembling. She's scared of the owl. Uh-oh! There goes that phone again. Here"—she gave the cat to Mick and got up quickly—"you hold her. I'd better get it."

Mick watched the sky fill with stars. The Big Dipper swung across it. In the clear and infinite darkness he could make out the small and fuzzy Pole Star. Sometimes, on a night like this, the northern lights could be seen flashing at the end of the horizon.

One night, Claudia had called him out to the deck of the studio to dance with her, accompanied only by the celestial music she alone could hear in the flaming ribbons of sky. He could see her now—waltzing alone in her white lace nightgown. Her head was thrown back, her eyes were closed, her lips were smiling, and her long fingers held the hem of her filmy gown. He took her in his arms and twirled around and around the deck with her.

The gentle swaying of the porch swing and Crosby's warm purring were lulling him, making him drowsy. It seemed as though a long time passed before he heard the screen door slam.

Penelope stood before him. She wasn't wearing her glasses, and Mick saw a shocked, dazed look in her eyes.

"Penelope, what's the matter?" he asked. "Who was that on the phone?"

"Chap," she whispered. Her voice was toneless and dead. "He said he's been trying to reach me for hours to tell me they arrested Sandy this afternoon for the murder of that girl."

Nine

"WHY, FOR CHRIST'S sake?"

Mick led Penelope to the swing. Her hand was cold and limp. Yet she walked stiffly beside him, as though if she relaxed a single muscle, she would crumple like a rag doll.

"They found a camera strap with Sandy's nametape sewed into it." Her voice remained flat and without expression. "It matched some dye on the girl's neck. They think it was used to kill her."

Mick recalled Caron's numerous questions about the camera strap that afternoon—those questions that had seemed so pointless at the time. He felt sick as he heard himself describing it. It was all too easy to visualize Penelope carefully and neatly sewing name tapes into all her daughter's possessions before she went off to college. He could also recall Reynolds asking him, was Mrs. Winslow's daughter sometimes called "Cassandra"? Claudia had always called her that. No doubt Penelope would have ordered Sandy's name tapes printed with her real name, in homage to the gravity of her only child's first great adventure in leaving home for the first time.

Now he understood the reason for the immediate end to his conversation with the two detectives after he'd described the camera strap around the girl's neck the night he first saw her.

Around her neck!

But it hadn't been anywhere near her body when he found it on Wrecker's Point. He was sure of that. Where had they found it? Had they found the camera as well?

"Hell, Penelope, that's not sufficient reason to arrest her. I'm sure Chap knows that. There must be some sort of mistake."

"I don't understand why they did, either." She looked at Mick with terror in her eyes. "Chap said there were a number of things he'll tell me when he sees me tomorrow. He's going to meet me at the ferry first thing in the morning to try and arrange for us to see her."

"I don't get it, Penelope." Mick shook his head in disbelief. "Caron and Reynolds seemed like a couple of smart cops. It's hard to believe they'd make an arrest on so little evidence."

She shivered. "Chap told me it was a god-awful mess—those were his exact words. Oh, I wish I could talk to her!"

Mick didn't know what to say. The situation was grotesque, and absurd, like everything about the girl's death. He felt a sudden overwhelming need to protect Penelope. She was frightened and vulnerable, nothing like the competent and composed woman he thought he knew. And, worst of all, he felt as though all the evidence that led the police to Sandy had been given by him.

Jesus, why had he ever come back? He somehow felt the girl wouldn't even have been on the island were it not for him, although he knew this made no sense at all.

"I'm going to get you some brandy and a sweater," he said.

He went to the kitchen cabinet where he'd noticed Penelope kept the liquor. After considerable rummaging around, he found a bottle of brandy in the back of the cabinet. It seemed obviously to be used only for cooking, spattered as it was with hardened drops of long-gone cake batters, its label soaked transparent by various butters and cooking oils. Mick sniffed the contents and took a good-sized swig before splashing some into a teacup. It was harsh and raw, but still contained plenty of alcohol. He grabbed a worn gray sweatshirt hanging on a hook in the mud room.

"Here, put this on," he said.

She turned her head away. "That's Sandy's." She spoke as though her daughter were dead.

"It was all I could find. Come on, put it on anyway." Mick draped the sweatshirt around Penelope's shoulders. She was trembling so much she couldn't hold the cup of brandy. He held it to her lips and she took a sip.

"He said there was a letter signed 'Cassandra' in the girl's pocket," she murmured.

"So Sandy did know her?"

"Maybe it was another Cassandra. That's possible, isn't it?"

"Oh, sure—maybe," he replied, vaguely.

But of course Sandy must have known the girl. Mick wondered why he hadn't guessed that immediately. That afternoon Sandy had asked him "Are you sure it was a Hasselblad?" He'd been surprised at the time that she'd ever heard of one. Then when she asked if the Botticelli painting he referred to was the nude standing on a seashell with flowers floating around her. What difference did that make? He remembered also how Sandy's questions had been followed by her abrupt and awkward departure immediately afterward. Yes, he'd noticed all those things at the time, yet thought nothing more of them.

"Did Chap tell you who the girl was?" he asked.

Penelope shrugged as though it didn't matter who she was— not now, anyway. "No one I knew. He said her name was Vanessa something—Berg, no, Bell, I think. Apparently she wasn't from around here, from South Carolina—Charleston—I think he said."

"I doubt if Vanessa Bell was her real name and I doubt if she was from Charleston, either," he said.

Penelope ignored his comment, put her face in her hands, and began to cry.

Mick was always uncomfortable with women's tears. He'd

been glad Claudia had seldom cried. He associated weeping with his mother and aunts—that trio of gloomy sisters who routinely offered up great chorales of sobs at the least provocation. He'd always felt such outbursts were in the category of menstrual blood, moon madness, childbed terrors, and other fearful female mysteries. Tears were something relating to the dark and secret life of women no man could fully understand or partake of.

"Don't cry, Penelope," he said helplessly. "Why don't you just go to bed now and try to get some sleep? There's nothing whatsoever you can do tonight."

The sweatshirt fell to the floor as she jumped up from the swing impatiently and went to the opposite end of the porch. She crossed her arms tightly around her chest, looked up at the starry sky, and let out a loud and passionate cry of grief and anger that seemed to go on resounding in the still night air.

Mick went over and put his arms around her. "I'm sorry. I didn't mean to speak in platitudes. Cry, yell all you want—do whatever makes you feel better."

Sobbing, she nodded her head obediently.

"I never should have told anyone about the girl taking my picture," he said gently, "never told them I saw her wearing that damned camera strap."

"They would have found it anyway."

"Maybe, but they might not have known it was hers."

"There's something else." Her voice shook. "Someone saw her car parked on Chapman's Hill that morning . . . "

"Oh Jesus!"

Mick heard himself saying to Reynolds, "Don't even attempt it unless you've got a four-wheel-drive vehicle."

He had been talking about the dirt road to the ruin of the old Chapman House Hotel, the nearest road that overlooked Wrecker's Point. Mick saw the raised letters—4WD TURBO—on Sandy's old Subaru's rusting rear door.

But he also recalled coming back to the house that afternoon, remembered the way Sandy had come running home, excited to tell her mother of what news she'd heard down at the harbor—

the rumor that Tom Girtin had finally shot someone he found trespassing among his beloved terns. It had struck him as such a childish thing to do—definitely not something anyone would do if she'd just that morning killed the person herself. At least not something someone who wasn't a mighty good actress would do. Mighty damned good. Sandy struck Mick as a somewhat simple and guileless girl. He was sure she couldn't have carried off an act like that.

"I don't know why Chap wouldn't tell me anything more. He just kept saying we'd discuss it in the morning," Penelope said. "Why does he have to be like that, always so sure of himself, always trying to be in control of everything?"

"I'm sure he's just unable to sort out what he needed to tell you tonight. After all, he's her father."

"You're right—oh, Mick, I shouldn't have gotten angry with him on the phone tonight. He adores her. I don't know why I did that—"

"Shhh. You didn't do anything wrong. Nothing wrong." He stroked her short hair tenderly, as one would a weeping child.

"That's probably why he didn't think we should discuss it anymore tonight—because I called him smug. I'm sure that's why he wouldn't tell me what the letter said. Or maybe he doesn't know. I didn't mean to sound as though I blamed him for not making them set her free. I mean, he's not a criminal attorney. If he could have, he would have, wouldn't he?"

"Of course," Mick murmured.

"Oh God! Poor Chap! Why wasn't I here when he first called today? Dear God, what can I do to help her? Oh God, my poor little girl—"

"I'm going to talk to Reynolds and Caron tomorrow." Mick spoke calmly to subdue her increasing hysteria. Were it not for that, he would certainly have expected her to respond sarcastically, demanding, with considerable justification, to know what the hell good that could possibly do.

Instead, she said eagerly, "Oh, yes, Mick, will you? Please talk to them."

Everything Penelope had told Mick indicated that, even if Sandy was innocent of the girl's death, she certainly knew her, and probably knew her very well. But that was all it proved. With the uncanny intuition he always used to have when he was painting well, Mick felt absolutely certain Cassandra Winslow was innocent . . .

But why the hell had she been arrested? The police didn't seem to have much to go on—a possession apparently belonging to Sandy that might have been the weapon, her car's presence near the scene of the crime at around the probable time. Did the letter in the girl's pocket indicate a motive?

He decided it must have.

Mick recalled the night he and Penelope had returned from Vinnie's. He saw the silent searchlights dancing, dipping, and endlessly scanning the beach and dunes. Again he heard those light footfalls on the road outside his room and saw once more that mysterious and menacing figure who loomed large, still and silent on the dark road—watching until the door of the house closed and the kitchen light went out.

The images came together. For the first time Mick comprehended that the footsteps had been Sandy's—that she must have surreptitiously gone down to the beach. The figure on the road had been Reynolds, who had followed her home. Her presence on the beach that night must have made the pair of detectives consider carefully any possible reasons she might have had for coming alone to check out the scene of the crime. Did they perhaps think she was looking for the murder weapon she had left behind?

Why the hell had the kid been crazy enough to do that? Didn't she know *anything*? Even he had remembered reading that murderers often returned to their victim's body—in fact, were often the first people police found there.

But if Sandy hadn't killed the girl—and she hadn't, any more than he had—who did?

Fog suddenly rolled in from the sea, enveloping the house and making the stars disappear. Its chill dampness forced Mick to become aware that his shirt was soaked with Penelope's tears.

78

He drew her closer, for warmth and more. As he did, he decided he wouldn't be leaving Dutchman's Island now.

He no longer wanted to.

And he couldn't. Not until he'd done everything possible to determine who *really* killed the girl on Wrecker's Point.

Ten

MICK HADN'T SLEPT all night.

It was still dark, but birds had already begun to sing in the bay-berry bushes. Pink streaks of dawn flooded outwards as the sun rose from the sea. He hid his face in the pillow and yanked the twisted sheet up around his head. The numerals on his watch told him it was quarter to five.

He got up, pulled down the shade, lay down in bed again, rolled over once more, and closed his eyes. But he couldn't stop thinking about last night.

It was easy for him to understand how his attempt to comfort Penelope had suddenly turned to desire. As he'd held her in his arms on the porch, Mick had become aware of her body against his. She hadn't resisted when he kissed her or began to unbutton her dress. And when she finally lay in bed beside him, she had said, with all the solemn gravity of truth, "Now I'll never be able to stop loving you, Mick. Never."

What a conceited bastard he'd been to answer, "Then don't— please don't!" He groaned at the memory of his remark, but at the same time, the thought of her skin touching his brought on a wave of yearning. How had he managed never to see how beautiful she was before last night?

He banged his fist angrily against the pillow, cursing whatever had made him do what he'd done. For he had destroyed their exquisite moment of climax by crying out, "Claudia!"

He hadn't been able to stop the word from coming. He'd begged Penelope to let him explain, but she'd only said with quiet dignity, "There's nothing to explain, Mick. I understand." She left his bed and returned to the house. When he tried to follow her, he found the door locked.

His head ached. He sat on the edge of the bed and stared at the braided rug lying on the linoleum floor. As he followed the graying strips in their monotonous spiral, Mick knew he *had* to do what he'd promised her last night—find out who really killed the girl who called herself Vanessa Bell. Even if it was impossible.

He pulled some clean clothes from his duffel, but as he started for the shower, he caught sight of Claudia smiling at him from a tarnished silver frame on the bureau. He opened the drawer and carefully placed the frame face-down inside.

After he'd showered and dressed, he stepped out the door. A robin was standing among the yellow dandelions on the lawn, already exulting the morning with song. The leaves of every green growing thing were dazzled with dew that captured and magnified the rays of sunlight while the coolness of evening still lingered.

He drove to the village. There was a pay phone down near the dock, where he telephoned the State Police, asking to speak with Detectives Reynolds or Caron. Neither was available, he was told, and he declined the operator's offer to connect him with someone else.

As he drove past Mrs. Pinkham's boarding house, he noticed the dusty brown sedan Reynolds had brought over on the ferry was parked outside. At least they hadn't left the island yet.

Mrs. Pinkham was up early, hanging her wash on the line. The wind was fresh and the white sheets flapped like the wings of some great seabird. An albatross, perhaps, Mick thought bitterly.

She jumped with surprise when he came up behind her. "You're Claudia Nichols's husband, aren't you?" She eyed him suspiciously. "Heard someone say you were back. Almost didn't recognize you. You sure do look a lot older."

Islanders always believed in speaking their mind.

"I suppose I must," Mick said. "It's been four years."

"Something I can do for you?" The smell in the air was a strange mixture of roses, seaweed, and Clorox.

"I was driving by and happened to notice Detective Reynolds's car. I take it he's still here?"

"The other one left, but yes—he's here."

"I wonder if you'd let him know I'd like to speak with him as soon as possible today?"

"No trouble. I expect I'll see him. He'll know where to reach you?"

"Yes. Thanks a lot, Mrs. Pinkham."

"As I said, no trouble."

A seagull lighted on the clothesline post as she finished putting clothespins in the sheet and began to hang up her faded towels. Sam Palmer's pickup truck pulled up to the boatyard, while Ry Pinkham ambled over to his grocery store to get ready for his few morning customers—putting the percolator on and setting out some of his wife's homemade doughnuts, so early passengers for the day's first ferry could get a cup of "some decent stuff," as he referred to his coffee.

As soon as Mick returned to the house, he went to the back door. Penelope was sitting at the kitchen table. She was wearing a dress of sun-faded blue cotton, sprinkled with flowers. He thought it would feel soft and smell of sunshine.

She opened the door, but said nothing until he put his arms around her and tried to draw her to him.

She pulled away. "No, Mick—don't."

She poured him a cup of coffee and put two slices of bread in the toaster. When Mick took a bite of toast, the crisp crunching sounded like an explosion in the heavy silence.

Finally he said, "I'm trying to find a way to tell you how sorry I am for what I said last night."

"There's no need to apologize." Her voice sounded cool and distant, the way it sometimes did. "We both got carried away. You felt sorry for me and I mistook your loneliness for something else. That's all. I made a fool of myself. It won't happen again." She brought her dishes to the sink and began to rinse them. "Mick, I think it would be best if you stayed at Mrs. Pinkham's for the next few days until you're ready to leave. I'll arrange it."

"I thought I told you last night I wasn't going—that I'd changed my mind."

"Yes, but you will leave," she said calmly. "And it will be better when you do."

"Why, for Christ's sake?"

"I don't think I need to explain why. The reason's obvious, isn't it?"

"You mean so we won't be tempted to make love again? Is that why?" He stood up and took her by the shoulders, turning her face to his. She looked away. "Penelope," he pleaded, "please listen to me. I don't understand why I can't escape Claudia. I only returned to the island to say a final good-bye to her, but Goddamn it, she won't let me!" His voice rose to a shout.

"You don't have to explain. Don't put yourself through this, please don't. Because I understand—really I do."

"No, I doubt that you do, Penelope. How could you? Because I sure as hell don't! Jesus! When I first saw your daughter on the ferry coming over, I thought she might be Claudia—just because she'd grown so tall and long-legged. And when I saw that exquisite girl coming out of the water that night, I thought she was Claudia, too. But the worst time was when I saw her lying dead on the beach. Did you know that? There was my beautiful, beloved Claudia—home at last! There she was, drowned off Wrecker's Point, washed ashore with seaweed tangled in her hair. No, but perhaps not drowned—perhaps alive—alive and given back to me!" He collapsed wearily into his chair. "Yeah, at that moment I knew I'd lost my mind, was hallucinating. But last night . . . I never expected to love another woman, didn't think I ever could. But you changed everything. I just wanted to be there for you, to be—to do—whatever you wanted or needed. I wanted to wake up this morning and find you sleeping in my arms. I still do." He reached across the table and took her hand in his.

She closed her eyes tight. "Last night was the most terrible and most beautiful night of my life," she whispered.

"Then won't you give this another chance? Please?"

She pulled her hand away and shook her head. "Mick, you must know how much I loved Claudia. She was my very dearest friend, and I'll think of her and miss her for some part of every day—always. I understand too well how you could never stop loving her . . . " She opened her eyes and he saw they were bright with tears. "But I can't be Claudia's surrogate, Mick. I just can't. Please understand that. I'd forever be comparing myself to her and forever finding myself lacking in your eyes."

Mick stared glumly at the meandering sepia specks of toast crumbs scattered across his plate, as Penelope rose to put the milk in the refrigerator. "I haven't forgotten what else I said last night," he said.

She was silent.

"Did you hear me, Penelope? Have you forgotten what I said I was going to do?"

"You mean find out who killed that girl?"

"Yes."

"Do you actually believe you can?" He detected irony in her tone.

"Well, I sure as hell am going to try. But just let me stay here until I do. I promise nothing will happen between us unless you want it to. Everything can be just as it was before last night, if that's what you really want. Friends—nothing more. But won't you let me, stay, Penelope? Not at Mrs. Pinkham's but here where I've been, over the garage?"

She nodded her head, looking down, avoiding his eyes.

Mick was surprised that he instantly felt the sort of adrenaline rush he always did when a fresh canvas was newly stretched, primed and waiting on his easel, while he chose his palette in preparation for a work long imagined but not yet begun. The ritual acts of craft—the careful choosing and neat laying out of tubes of color, the selecting of the precise brushes—always helped to prepare him for the task of seizing and organizing images to transform them into a work of art. He found it strange, but somehow comforting, that this unlikely challenge felt the same.

"Listen, Penelope," he said. "I'm sure Sandy knew her. You know that, don't you?"

She looked at him with terror in her face. Mick realized at that moment that she hadn't the same absolute certainty he had that her daughter was innocent.

"Just because she knew her doesn't mean she killed her," he added.

She nodded. It was a sweet and solemn, childlike nod that tore his heart out. "It looks that way. But I certainly never heard of her."

"Do you remember when I said Vanessa Bell wasn't the girl's real name? Or that she probably wasn't from Charleston?"

"Yes."

"Well, you've heard of Vanessa Bell, I'm sure. Charleston, too—the English one."

"No. Should I have?" Penelope seemed puzzled.

Mick realized his art historical references weren't at all clear to her just because they would have been to Claudia.

"Vanessa Bell was an English painter, a founder of the Omega Workshops and Virginia Woolf's sister. She was close friends with Roger Fry—the whole Bloomsbury set. She become a cult figure among a number of my female students in London, especially those involved in feminist consciousness-raising and obsessed with earlier art by women. Hers was a name a more sophisticated classmate of Sandy's might well have chosen as a disguise."

Now Penelope was paying careful attention to what he said.

"Anyway, Vanessa Bell lived in a farmhouse outside London

with the great love of her life—a man she left her husband for. He was a well-known painter named Duncan Grant. They decorated every inch of their love nest—every piece of furniture in it, too—with their paintings, mostly Vanessa's. It was her masterpiece. Today, it's a small museum—I've been there. Their life together was idyllic, almost perfect, except for one fact. Duncan Grant, although he adored Vanessa, was also homosexual. In fact, he was in love with her husband."

Penelope raised her eyebrows skeptically.

"Can you guess what their house was called?" he continued.

"Charleston?" she replied, dubiously.

"You've got it! Don't you agree with me now that it has to be a phony name?"

"Well, I'll admit your idea is somewhat convincing."

"The big question is, why did the girl come out here to the island under an assumed name? And where's the damned camera that was attached to that strap? I'm sure the police never found it." Mick tapped his fingers impatiently on the table. "I've got to find out who she really was."

Penelope nodded once more. Mick couldn't help observing that her lips resembled the ripe strawberries that grew in her garden—red and full and sweet—but he forced himself to concentrate on gathering from her whatever information he needed.

"Has it seemed to you that anything might be troubling Sandy lately?"

"I don't know. Maybe . . . "

"What do you mean?" Mick spoke gently, sensing her hesitation.

"It's just that since she came home this summer, it has seemed odd to me that she's had nothing to say about school—her teachers, other kids, her assignments, how the exams went—nothing at all. I have to admit she clams up whenever I bring up any of these things and manages to change the subject."

"That wasn't like her?"

"No, not at all." Penelope's tone was emphatic.

"Did she have a lot of friends?"

"Well, as many as island kids can. After all, there aren't that many of them out here. She and Paula Potter have been best friends since kindergarten. And then there's Johnny Selcott, although recently he seems to have become more than that."

"I meant friends from school."

"She never mentioned any particular one, but that didn't really surprise me. She was meeting so many new people, I think she might have been somewhat overwhelmed. And don't forget, with both Johnny and Paula at State U., close by, she was still able to see a lot of them. At Christmastime she talked mostly about her classes, her teachers, the museum—" Penelope's voice broke and she hid her face in her hands. But she quickly gained control of herself after taking a deep breath and gazing steadily for a moment out the window behind him at the high horizon. Mick noticed for the first time that her eyes were green, and somewhat slanted, like a cat's. "Last night Chap told me she's been like that lately with him, too."

"Did he have any idea why?"

"No, but, after all—that's Chap. He rarely lets his imagination run away with him."

Sunlight struck the curls framing her face. Her fair skin was transparent with fatigue. Faint lavender shadows beneath her eyes lent a look of fragile spirituality to her beauty. "You look like a Fra Angelico angel," he whispered. "When all this is over, when Sandy is home again, will you let me take you to Florence?"

Mick was suddenly glad he'd never visited Italy with Claudia. He could visualize Penelope's delicate coloring shimmering like coral and burnished gold against the dark and virile stonework of Florence. He wanted to take her to the temples at Paestum, to show her the crumbling Baroque village outside Palermo where his mother was born, to see Penelope's golden curls shimmering in the pastel light of a Venetian canal. He wanted them to toast their newfound love with tiny cups of black coffee sitting under the dappled green of some gnarled and ancient grape arbor.

She blushed, but otherwise ignored his comment. "I thought

the only reason for her recent secretiveness was because she didn't want me to guess what was going on between her and Johnny."

Mick suddenly glanced at the clock on the kitchen wall. "God, Penelope—look what time it is! You'd better hurry if you want to catch that ferry."

He noticed how her hands shook when she opened her purse to count her money. He yearned to take her in his arms, to assure her that everything would be all right. But he couldn't. Everything wasn't all right, and now she again wore that poignant look of dread.

He followed her out to her car. She put the key in the ignition, then turned to him and said, "Mick?"

"Yes?"

"No matter how it ended last night, I meant everything I said. Nothing can ever change that."

Before he could respond, she fastened her seat belt and drove away.

Eleven

THE PHONE AT the cottage rang again and again with no answer.

Mick decided Trudy hadn't yet returned. But when he'd seen her board the small plane, she had been alone, convincing him that Evgeny Otkresta was likely to still be on the island.

He was sure he'd caught a brief glimpse of him from the kitchen window a half hour or so ago. Evgeny had been walking around the cottage purposefully, as though he was looking for someone or something.

Mick suspected that the young Russian, with his limited and heavily accented English, preferred to avoid answering the telephone. He decided it was better to surprise him with an unexpected visit anyway.

He crossed the stone wall and followed a short path through the bushes up to the lawn of the cottage. He rang the brass ship's bell hanging by the front door, but there was no response. When he tried the back door, he found it unlocked, as doors on the island usually were.

Inside the kitchen, he saw an assortment of glasses and coffee cups on the sink and counter. Dark rings of coffee or wine had formed in most of the vessels, indicating none had been used that morning. The house had a profound silence.

He crept up the stairs silently. It wasn't difficult to determine which of the upstairs bedrooms was Evgeny's. The floor of one large and sunny dormer room was littered with clothes more suitable for a rock star than a painter. Gallery catalogues littered the unmade bed. Mick picked two up, then tossed them down again. He wasn't surprised to find one was for a recent Basquiat exhibit in a gallery in Zurich, the other for new works on paper by Rauschenberg in New York. Mick saw purple stains from a blueberry muffin on the linen sheets and found a sketch pad buried under the blanket. He flipped through it, saw that Evgeny's few drawings were clumsy and awkward but nevertheless had a certain brutal energy that might have made a trained eye such as Trudy's feel he would grow into something, in time. Most of the drawings were of cats—smudged and reworked to death with an HB pencil.

One door in the long hallway led to a small utility room where an open ironing board stood with an unplugged iron on it. A gray silk caftan hung from a laundry tree, as though Trudy had first thought of wearing it, then changed her mind.

A floorboard creaked as Mick stepped on it, and he involuntarily started, but the house remained eerily silent. He was about to leave the room when he noticed a door to a narrow storage closet, with a combination padlock on it.

Some sudden urge made him want to unlock it, although he knew he wasn't likely to find Evgeny hiding in its narrow space. He didn't know why he felt certain it contained, not linens, but leftover bits and pieces of those summers long past when Claudia had lived with her aunt at the cottage.

He tried a combination of numbers composed of the date of his and Claudia's wedding anniversary, but those didn't open the lock—nor did a combination based on the date of the day they met. Remembering that this door had probably been locked before she met him, he next tried a combination based on her birthday, and this time the lock sprang open.

Inside the small and shallow closet were shelves with numerous boxes of assorted sizes neatly piled on all but one, which was full of books. Mick pulled a heavy volume out at random and immediately realized it was Claudia's yearbook from Vassar.

He'd never known what she looked like in those days before he met her. It didn't take long to find her graduation picture. Her expression in it was grave and scholarly, giving no hint of the radiant smile he had discovered that morning in London six years ago. The silent room was suddenly filled with Claudia's presence, although he could neither hear nor see her.

He slammed the book shut and put it back on the shelf, but another one found its way into his hand. This was a pale lemon yellow French paperback, its pages the characteristic ragged, handcut ones—the title set in classically restrained and elegant Garamond. The author was Colette. Mick opened it and saw the handwriting on the flyleaf: "Claudia L. Nichols." Her place was still marked by a snapshot of Sam Palmer. Sam was much younger in the photograph and wore no beard. He was even more good-looking than Mick would have guessed. He sat in the stern of a sailboat, holding the sheet and tiller, smiling intimately at whoever took the picture. Perhaps the boat was *Felicity*—Mick couldn't be certain—but he knew the photograph was Claudia's and that Sam's smile was a lover's smile, intimate, adoring.

He placed the book back on the shelf. His hands were shaking. He shut the door and snapped the padlock shut. The closet had a ghostly, haunted smell he noticed for the first time. It was the smell of old paper, old dust, secrets, and spiderwebs. He didn't want to come near it ever again.

He climbed a flight of narrow steps to the window's walk that crowned the shingle roof. From inside, the small tower had a 360-degree-angle view of all the land surrounding the house. Claudia had told him of happy hours she used to spend up there, reading and daydreaming. He looked in each direction, but saw no one.

Downstairs, the dining room also revealed nothing. It appeared unused. The handsome mahogany shutters were drawn to keep the sun from fading a well-framed set of watercolors—early LeBruns.

91

When Mick entered the vast living room, he saw that the Russian painter's *Homage to Vladimir Ilych* still stood in the same place, warring with the cheerful and sunlit oils by Aunt Betsy that hung, tastefully and expensively framed, on every wall.

Trudy's telephone number at her apartment in New York was prominently displayed by the phone. Mick sat down and dialed. He heard a car outside, and from the window he saw a light blue Volvo sedan turn out from the dirt road and drive toward town. He remembered Penelope telling him she'd had a chance to speak to Meer about the studio, and decided the car must belong to his other tenant since the dirt road led to only three houses—Penelope's, his own studio, and the cottage.

Just as he was about to hang up, Trudy's capable assistant answered the phone and told him Trudy had flown to South Dakota for the unveiling of a major installation and performance piece by the up-and-coming young Sioux artist, Jay Good Bird. She wasn't expected back until day after tomorrow. She would probably spend a day or two in the city working on the article she was writing about Good Bird, then return to the island. No, the assistant couldn't help him, she was afraid. She knew nothing of Evgeny's whereabouts.

As she spoke, telling Mick more than he wanted to know, his eyes wandered in ennui to Evgeny's large collage painting.

Finally he said, "Thanks, anyway. If you should hear from him, you can reach me at this number. There's an answering ma—oh my God!"

"Are you all right?" the assistant asked.

"Yes. I mean, good-bye." He hung up the phone quickly and looked again at the lower-right corner of the work.

Something new had been inserted: a photograph of the dead girl, posing nude against a background of white seamless paper where crudely drawn, childlike waves of an imaginary ocean had been added. Flowers floated through the air. On looking closer, Mick saw that the photograph was actually a montage of several photographs, somewhat after the manner of David Hockney's Polaroids. The montages constructing the figure had themselves

been montaged onto a grainy and much-enlarged image of a scallop shell. The sweet expression of the original had been replaced
by a vapid and somehow sinister half-smile.

Obviously the girl on the beach had reminded someone other
than Mick of Botticelli's *Venus* as she rose from the sea.

He tore the photograph from the canvas and stuffed it in his
pocket.

Twelve

MICK RAN UP the gangplank just in time to board the eleven o'clock ferry before it sailed. He saw the brown sedan parked behind a truck on the lower deck, and soon located Reynolds sitting in the sun up in the bow. His eyes were closed as he absorbed the warmth of the sunlight.

Mick sat down beside him on the bench.

"I see you got my note," the policeman said quietly. "Good."

"I'm glad you left it on my door," Mick said. "I didn't think we'd be able to connect. I was told you'd already left the island."

"Yes—I had checked out of the rooming house earlier this morning," Reynolds said. "But I strolled around for a while. I missed the earlier ferry, but fortunately heard from Mrs. Pinkham that you had telephoned for me." He smiled. "A fortuitous coincidence. What can I do for you, Mr. Merisi?"

So you don't consider the case closed yet, Mick thought. Otherwise it wouldn't have been important to meet with me.

"I've got some information for you," Mick murmured.

"I see." Reynolds said thoughtfully, then waited.

The boat vibrated noisily as the powerful propellers started churning. It was better not to try and talk until the ferry had moved out of the channel into the open sea, Mick decided. He looked around. There appeared to be no one besides the two of them on deck. Inside the enclosed cabin he saw a ponytailed young man getting a cup of coffee from the machine—probably the driver of the truck—but no one he knew.

Off to starboard a lobster boat bobbed cheerfully on the waves. Its solitary captain and crew waved to the ferry as it passed and caused the smaller boat to wallow in the wide wake. The lobster boat reminded Mick of a bathtub toy he'd had as a child, its playful and jaunty lines so bright and freshly painted—an idyllic vision, which from this distance and downwind gave no hint of the rotten smell aboard.

"Can I get you a cup of coffee?" Reynolds asked.

"No, thanks."

"Mind if I get myself one?" Without waiting for an answer the detective went inside and soon returned with steaming coffee with milk—the color of the island's clay cliffs that were now receding into the distant horizon. Mick wished Evgeny Otkresta's scarlet kite would suddenly rise into the sky, until he remembered seeing it the other day, torn and fallen into the brush.

"I guess you know why I wanted to talk to you?" Mick said, when Reynolds was again seated beside him.

"I've got an idea."

Mick felt his throat grow tight with anger. Why the hell was the guy so calm? Did police work so immunize you against tragedy it was impossible to grasp what the arrest of this young girl meant—what it would do to her young life—to her mother's life?

"Why did you arrest Cassandra Winslow?" Mick asked. "Anyone could see she's not the kind of person who could murder anyone. I mean, just look at her—"

Reynolds turned to face him, frowning slightly. "Exactly what have you been told about the situation, Mr. Merisi? Nothing has been released to the press, so I assume you're going by information obtained from a private source."

"Just what her mother told me last night, that Cassandra's been arrested for the murder of the girl I discovered on the beach. The girl who was going by the alias of Vanessa Bell."

Reynolds sighed, then drank some coffee. Mick said nothing more while waiting for him to speak. "It's interesting that you say the name is an alias. We're still awaiting dental records, fingerprints, all that—anything to try and make certain of the victim's identity. But that's the only name we've turned up so far. She was registered at Mrs. Pinkham's under that name." His voice dropped. "I'll try to define our situation for you."

"However you want to do it. I just want to know what the hell is going on."

"Mr. Merisi, there is little any police officer dreads as much as a false confession. I'm sure you can understand why. Valuable time is lost, possibly allowing the real perpetrator to get away. The department loses credibility should the confession later prove to be false. No, contrary to what the public believes, the police do not ever want to make an arrest of the wrong person, even if that person confesses to a crime. There are, however, certain criteria to be met in determining—"

"Are you trying to tell me she confessed to it? Oh, come on! I don't believe this crap!"

"Mr. Merisi, please let me continue." Reynolds set his empty coffee cup down on the deck. "I'm trying to give you whatever information I can," he murmured. "Let's do it my way, okay?"

"Okay. Sorry. Go on."

"Assuming these criteria—and they are quite specific—are met, the police have no choice but to make an arrest. Am I making myself clear?"

"I'm afraid so. But if the kid was crazy enough to confess to something she didn't do, what next? She probably told you something she'd heard from me, something no one else knew."

Reynolds shook his head. "No, she didn't."

"But aren't you guys at all open to finding out who really did it? Let's put it another way. Suppose I were to find the real killer—"

"Do you think you can?" There was the ghost of an ironic smile on Reynolds's lips.

"Well, I'm sure as hell going to try. Look"—now it was Mick who was whispering—"I told you, or Jerry Francis—I don't remember which—that I'm pretty sure I saw a Russian guy named Evgeny Otkresta meeting the girl on the beach the night I first saw her. Do you remember my saying that? About someone hiding in the shadow of the bluffs that night?"

Reynolds said nothing.

"Okay. Otkresta's a house guest of a tenant of mine, Trudy Glass. This morning I went alone into the cottage she rents from me—"

Reynolds raised his eyebrows. "It is all too true that an amateur sleuth has certain freedoms the police lack—freedom to enter a domain without a search warrant, for example." He smiled.

"Well, let's admit I went in uninvited. Let's just say I'm the landlord and I needed to fix a leaky faucet. Anyway, there's this painting—a construction, collage, actually—the guy's working on. I noticed he'd added an interesting detail since I saw it the other day."

"Such as?"

"Remember I said the girl looked like a particular painting, the Botticelli *Birth of Venus?* It was the only way I could accurately describe her. The resemblance was quite uncanny."

Reynolds nodded. "I do remember. And I'm familiar with the painting. I would agree it was an accurate description."

"I assumed that was just my lousy habit of seeing everything in terms of some damned painting or other—my wife used to kid me about it . . . "

Don't think about Claudia, not now, he reminded himself.

"Anyway, I thought you might find this interesting." He pulled the photograph he'd taken off the *Homage to Vladimir Ilych* that morning.

"I found this picture pasted onto a collage Evgeny Otkresta's working on." Mick watched the policeman's face for some reaction to the picture of the dead girl, or to what he had just said, but saw none. "I saw the particular work I'm speaking of in the living room of my other house on the island the same day I discovered the girl's body. I'd just stopped off to say hello to Trudy Glass; she's an old friend of mine and a patron of this painter. I got a damned good look at Otkresta's piece. This sure as hell wasn't there then."

Reynolds studied the crumpled picture. "May I keep it?"

"Yes."

Reynolds stood up and walked over to the railing. Mick followed him. Sachem Light was now visible on the horizon. About another forty-five minutes before they docked.

"You'll make good use of it, won't you?" Mick asked.

"I'll try to. You know, I've got a great deal of sympathy for Captain Francis." Reynolds changed the subject.

"Oh Christ! What the hell does a nut like Jerry Francis have to do with this, anyway? I thought it was great when you two guys stepped in and took over. Hell! That idiot was even acting like I did it."

Reynolds ignored his outburst. "As I said, a great deal of sympathy. It was unfortunate in many ways that Tony Caron was assigned this case, what with the somewhat irrational, even pathological rivalry Captain Francis has always felt when working with him—"

"What are you saying?"

"Only that yesterday Captain Francis put in his resignation, effective immediately. A replacement officer came to the island this afternoon."

Mick smelled cigarette smoke and noticed the other passenger had come outside on deck.

"Say," said Reynolds, pointing to Sachem Light, "that's quite a beautiful lighthouse over there, don't you agree? I've always been fascinated by lighthouses. You wouldn't happen to know when that one was built, would you?"

Mick shook his head.

The ponytailed young man tossed his cigarette into the sea and went back inside.

"Go on with what you were telling me," Mick said.

"I find it interesting that, once out of the force, police officers are quite willing to discuss matters that should remain confidential. There is nothing we can do to prevent it, of course. Regrettable, but true."

So that was it—Mick understood what Reynolds was saying. Don't ask me the details, ask him.

A few moments passed with neither speaking. The silence was interrupted by the ferry's four loud blasts warning a couple of laughing kids who were water-skiing to stay out of its wake.

Mick realized that now he was free to ask Jerry Francis as much as he wished about the case, and Jerry would probably talk—just to get back at his hated rival. And there was another reason. He, too, desired Penelope Winslow, and it was her daughter they would be speaking of. Yes, Jerry would tell him a lot he needed to know.

As they passed the lighthouse and approached the harbor, more boats surrounded them—trawlers, sailboats, motorboats, yachts. When the ferry pulled up to the dock, Reynolds took out his wallet and handed Mick his card. "I can always be reached at home," he said casually, as though they were two strangers who'd met on the boat, some salesman making the brief acquaintance of a potential client, although who played which part, Mick could not be sure.

"Then you will work with me? You'll pay attention to whatever I find out, check into it further?"

"So far as I'm able to," Reynolds said gravely, and Mick knew a deal had been struck.

He walked off the ferry onto the dock and watched the detective drive away. It was hot and steamy here on the mainland. The dock smelled of petroleum and fish—nothing like the clear, fresh island air. Mick wondered how he could kill an hour productively until the ferry sailed again.

Once more he asked himself, where was Evgeny Otkresta?

C H A P T E R

Thirteen

MICK NOTICED THAT, as usual, the Clam Bar was nearly empty. Only Jack Selcott and Sam Palmer were sitting at a table in the back, which was littered with papers, while the two of them drank coffee. It appeared to be a business meeting of some sort. They formed a solid and silent composition that had the grandeur of Cézanne's *Card Players*.

As he had hoped, Jerry soon walked in. Mick joined him at the bar and ordered a Bass Ale. "I'd like to talk to you about something," he said quietly, as soon as Vinnie left to go to the kitchen. "But not here."

"About the Winslow kid?" Jerry muttered.

"That's right. No one else knows about it yet, do they?"

"I don't think so. If they do, they sure as hell didn't hear it from me. Those other two bastards, though, no telling what they'd do to get their names in the paper."

"Can you come over to the house?" Mick asked. "We can talk there. No one's around. Penelope took the early ferry."

"Gotcha!" Jerry said morosely, and took a large gulp of his martini. "Did you know I quit the force?"

"I heard a rumor to that effect."

"Shit, it's time, man. Yep—way past time."

Mick paid his tab and left. He hoped Jerry wouldn't have any more to drink, for he was already entering the self-pitying stage. All it might take would be another of Vinnie's double straight-up martinis and the bartender's conviviality to make Jerry start talking about Sandy's arrest. Eventually, Mick knew, the story would come out—at least in mainland papers. The islanders, on the other hand, would gossip furtively among themselves but do all they could to keep it from becoming common knowledge else-where. Their history as wreckers had given them a character sus-picious of all outsiders, yet usually standing by one of their own against the world. Besides, they were so dependent upon summer tourism, they wouldn't want to reveal in any way that the island was less than a bucolic paradise—hardly a place where beautiful young visitors were murdered while innocently photographing the island's wildlife.

Mick sat on the porch, awaiting Jerry's arrival. He couldn't stop thinking of how sweet Penelope had looked as she sat in the fading twilight doing her needlepoint.

As soon as Jerry got there, he wasted no time in asking, "How'd you find out?"

"Chap Winslow called Penelope last night, and I was helping her in the garden at the time. She was very upset, and told me about it."

"Poor girl, she probably needed to talk to someone. She should have called me."

Mick let that pass. "What I don't understand is why? From what Penelope told me, you guys found this camera strap with a name tape of Sandy's sewed into it. Right?" He decided not to re-veal that he'd already heard from Reynolds Sandy had confessed.

"Right."

"Where'd they find it? I didn't see it when I discovered the body."

"The little kid had it."

"Then she must have seen the body before I did."

"No, she said she didn't. She found the strap way up in the dunes. She showed us where."

Mick remembered seeing what he thought was a red bandanna in Cathy's pocket as she walked back to the farmhouse—some beachcombing bit of treasure, a gaudy, pretty trinket to a child. Had the terns carried it up there into the dunes as decoration for their bare nests?

"How do you know the girl hadn't dropped it there herself, taking pictures?"

"Because there was dye on her neck that matched the dye in the strap, and blood that was the victim's blood type. It had been in saltwater, too. We never found a camera to go with it."

"So she was strangled?"

"No. Looks like there had been a struggle in the water. Whoever did it tightened the strap around her neck, trying to choke her." Jerry demonstrated dramatically. "There were plenty of rope burns, abrasions, cuts, but they didn't kill her. Instead, the killer pulled her underwater, held her there until she drowned."

"Wasn't she raped? I remember her fly was unzipped."

Jerry grunted. "No evidence of it—no semen, no hairs. Nope, the girl wasn't raped, but it looks like someone wanted to make it seem like she was. I've seen that happen before . . . "

"Are you saying the killer might be a woman trying to make it appear to be a man?"

"You're catching on, Merisi. Yeah, that's exactly what I think."

"How about Reynolds and Caron? Do they agree?"

"You don't happen to know where she keeps the booze, do you?"

Mick poured Jerry some gin and vermouth splashed over ice, and himself a Scotch. "This won't compare with Vinnie's martinis, but it's the best I can come up with."

"Thanks. How come you want to know all this, anyway, Merisi? I mean, it sure takes the heat off you."

"Penelope Winslow was my wife's closest friend. And the kid—Claudia loved her like her own. Anyway, I was asking earlier, how about Reynolds and Caron? Did they think the killer was a woman?"

Jerry grinned again. "What are you asking, Merisi? You want me to really tell you what they thought?"

"Yes." Mick gazed steadily at Jerry.

"Well, the truth is, Tony still thought you were the one worth watching, last I heard. And Reynolds, I don't think he'd decided anything yet. Quiet son of a bitch." He let out his belt a notch, and took a deep breath.

"So what made them think it was Sandy?"

"Penelope didn't tell you?"

"She said her car had been seen on Chapman Hill Road, that, plus the camera strap, and some note in the girl's pocket."

Jerry laughed contemptuously. "A note that said something to the effect of 'I could kill you for what you are doing. Sincerely, Cassandra.' Not a hell of a lot of Cassandras out there, are there?"

Oh, Jesus—Penelope didn't tell me what it said, Mick thought.

"When do they think the girl was killed?" he asked quietly.

"Between seven and eleven o'clock that morning."

"What about the Russian? Remember, I told you how I thought I saw him that night?"

"Couldn't have been him. Looks like he had an alibi for that morning. He was down at Palmer's buying a kite."

"The whole time?" Mick asked. "I mean, it wouldn't take three hours to buy a kite, for Christ's sake."

Jerry shrugged. "I didn't talk to him, Reynolds did. He seemed satisfied with his alibi, but he's a cold fish. You never know what he's thinking. Anyway, Merisi, we're talking about things that don't matter one goddamned bit under the circumstances."

"I don't understand what you're saying."

"Didn't Penelope tell you?"

"Tell me what?"

"That the kid confessed. Tony wanted to question her—and all of a sudden, she came right out and said she did it. I wasn't there, but he bought it. I hate that bastard's guts, but he's no dope."

"What?" Mick tried to appear surprised.

"That's right." Jerry grinned smugly. "Hell of a ticket, isn't it?"

"Couldn't it have been someone from off the island? I mean, I assume you've checked out the ferries, the airport, all that?" Mick asked.

"Sure did," said Jerry. "Took care of it myself. The girl came over here on Saturday afternoon. She and the Russian were the only people on the ferry. Seemed like they hit it off right away— or so I heard from one of the boys in the crew."

"I took it upon myself to try to talk with him this morning," Mick said. "He wasn't around. Has he left the island?"

"Nope. I've been checking every flight, every ferry. The fat bitch left the other day, but her boy-toy didn't. Not unless he swam. You ought to talk to Reynolds. He was the only one of us sort of interested in your idea that the Russian might be the one to look into." Jerry lit a cigarette, took a few puffs, and settled back comfortably in the chair. "I've been trying to give up these damned coffin nails for years. I'm down to only about ten a day—give or take a few."

Mick wasn't listening. I've got to talk to Trudy, he thought, got to find out what was going on that night at Vinnie's, why she slapped the girl.

"You know, Merisi, I've been in this crap game a long time." Jerry blew a smoke ring. "I've seen people kill who you never dreamed could do it. Yep, I've seen it happen more than once."

"What are you saying, Jerry?"

"Just that the Winslow kid might have done it. Why not? She said she did. Look, no one else left any traces around the body. No one else wrote the girl a letter threatening to kill her." Again he wore that smug smile.

"Then you *do* think Sandy did it?"

"Let's just say I'm glad I'm out of it. Listen, you won't tell Penelope what I said, will you? I'm damned fond of that lady. Wouldn't want her blaming me for this mess."

"I'm not planning to tell her."

"Look, Merisi, I don't understand your game. What's in it for you, anyway?" Jerry squinted as he studied Mick, his lips pursed, his breathing loud. "You're not fucking Penelope, are you?"

Mick jumped up and grabbed him by the collar. "I haven't hit anyone since I was fourteen years old, but I'm going to break my record pretty damned quick, if you don't get the hell out of here!"

Fourteen

MICK SPIT SAND from his mouth and groaned as he pulled himself up to a kneeling position. He reached up to feel his cheek where it stung and found his fingers were stained with blood.

He stood up and looked behind him. There it lay—that damned rusting misplaced mushroom mooring half buried in rocks and sand, all that was left of some forgotten boat lost at sea. He kicked at it angrily, adding a sore toe to his other injuries. In disgust he turned and limped away from Wrecker's Point.

Offshore he saw the bobbing lights of a fishing boat shrouded in the mist of a warm evening and shrunken moon. The roving beam from the west lighthouse swung around again, momentarily illuminating both sea and shore, but revealing nothing— although just what he'd expected to find, Mick didn't know. He'd been crazy to come down there with no flashlight. Crazy to come down there at all. The police had certainly combed the area by now.

He edged his way carefully around slippery pebbles, driftwood, and boulders. The tide was nearly high, with water covering most of the flat, smooth sand. He decided to take off his shoes and wade through the shallow edge of the incoming tide, avoiding those obstacles further up above the tideline. There was no surf that night, only gentle lapping at the shore. As he stepped into the water, it occurred to him that someone else could have walked from Wrecker's Point that same way, leaving no trace of their journey.

He heard a dog bark. Something about that sentinel sound at night always made him uneasy. He looked up toward the studio as a tall figure stepped out on the deck, looked around, then went back inside.

That must be Meer, Mick thought.

Hearing Stubbs bark reminded him again that Crosby hadn't been home the last two nights. He whistled for her as he walked up the dirt road toward the house, but she didn't come darting out of the bayberry. He wondered if a steady diet of field mice and moonlit dances with her feral cousins hadn't lured her away from his depressed and predictable dullness.

He tried to sort out the fragments of knowledge he'd acquired in the last two days. He'd found out from Mrs. Pinkham that the girl had arrived on the island with no luggage except the beach bag she kept with her always. No one had ever visited her. The telephone sitting in the front parlor of the boarding house had been silent, and the girl had left no evidence of her presence in the small room she rented on the top floor. The landlady commented approvingly that she had paid a full week's rent in advance—in cash. Like most islanders, Mrs. Pinkham mistrusted checks and refused to accept credit cards. Mick suspected she kept her cash from the "rents," as she called her boarders, in a sock hidden under the bed, or buried, like wreckers' secret treasure, in the backyard.

"Neatest, cleanest young lady I ever saw," Mrs. Pinkham had said. "Usually they leave makeup and all kinds of junk all over the place. But not this one. No, sir. She was neat as a pin," she emphasized, her admiration for this rare trait evident in her tone of voice.

But where she went each day and night, Mrs. Pinkham had no idea.

Mick was sure the police had never found her bag, for he believed that somewhere in that bag her real identity was revealed. That, and perhaps more.

When he reached the house, he glanced through the window into Penelope's small office. The red light of the answering machine was blinking urgently, but when he played back the message, it wasn't from her. Instead, it was from Trudy's assistant in New York, asking him to call as soon as possible. Mick immediately dialed the number she'd left, thinking that Evgeny had, at last, turned up or contacted her in some way.

She answered on the first ring, but the news she had was not about Evgeny. Instead, she told Mick that Trudy was in a hospital in South Dakota, after suffering a major stroke in the middle of Good Bird's performance piece. The girl's voice sounded tight and choked with tears. As she asked him if he'd located Evgeny yet, and he had to answer no, it occurred to him with sadness that this young woman was the closest thing to a child Trudy had. While he spoke, Mick looked out the window at the cottage, looming large and dark on the rise across the road. If anyone was there, they hadn't turned on a single light.

"I'll go over to the cottage and take a look, see if he's around," he said.

"I've been trying there all evening. The little punk has probably found someone else to mother him. When I think of the grief he's given her these past months—and she's been so good to him." She paused to gain control of herself. "I'm sorry. He's not one of my favorite people."

"It's okay," said Mick. "He affected me that way, too. God, I'm so damned sorry to hear about Trudy. Can I send flowers or something?"

"I'm not sure—she's in the ICU. I'm sorry, Mick, I can't talk now. I've got a number of other calls to make. Good-bye, and please—you *will* call me right back if you find Evgeny?"

"Sure," he said, without conviction. There was a click at the other end of the line and she was gone.

Mick suddenly needed to hear Penelope's voice, but when he dialed her room at the Holiday Inn near the prison, there was no answer. He decided she was probably having dinner with Chap again. The two of them were trying to figure out a way to make their daughter come to her senses, for Penelope had told Mick she and her ex-husband were now in total agreement that Sandy must be going through some sort of a nervous breakdown. Nothing else accounted for her bizarre behavior.

He remembered to bring a flashlight to light his path as he walked over to the cottage. As he expected, nothing in the house had changed since he'd been in there the other day. The same dirty cups and glasses were cluttered in and around the kitchen sink. Evgeny's unmade bed had not been slept in and his large assemblage still stood, an eerie presence in the dark living room.

He stepped down from the porch and saw globes of glowing green hidden among the rugosa roses. Claudia would have said they were fairy lanterns—that supernatural phosphorescent firelight only the bewitched could see.

"Crosby?" he said softly, but none of the green eyes belonged to her.

He slowly climbed the steps to his room over the garage, feeling lonely and depressed. He could taste dried blood that had dripped to his lips from the cut on his cheekbone. His wrists and palms ached from trying to break his earlier fall into the rocks and sand.

Nothing he'd found out so far formed a design of any sort. He wanted to discern some pattern that would help him pull the disconnected images together until they formed a balanced and inevitable composition.

Mick recalled a time when he had been confounded and frustrated after staring helplessly for days at the monotonous horizontals of the painting standing on his easel. He had painted in and then scraped out numerous ideas, none of which worked.

As he had gazed out the picture window, hoping his motif of

the ever-changing light on the sea would offer some solution, he noticed Claudia had left a silver cylinder of Clinique lipstick on the windowsill. A brief shaft of sunlight hit it.

In that instant, Mick saw exactly what was needed. He had mixed a pale and silvery gray, then painted a slender column along the left edge of the canvas. A thin diagonal slash of emerald and white touched the gray and ghostly vertical.

A window frame? Claudia's silver lipstick case? An empty vase?

It didn't matter. Suddenly the whole painting sang. The flat two-dimensionality of the canvas took on the grandeur of real space, that space his idol, Cézanne, had taught him could be invoked through color.

Mick hadn't added another brush stroke. The painting was complete.

Yes, he understood too well how much he needed some new vision—the sort of thing Claudia's accidentally placed tube of lipstick had been—to tie the present mass of sensations together. But time mattered, too, in this design. Mick had counted on Trudy Glass to help him understand the dead girl's relationship with her and Evgeny. Now she was silenced, perhaps forever. Besides himself and Sandy, Mrs. Pinkham and Vinnie, no one else on the island seemed to have had anything to do with the mysterious and solitary girl.

Except whoever killed her.

Fifteen

HE STUMBLED OVER the body lying in the sand, but when he looked behind him, it had disappeared.

Someone was washing the cut on his cheek with iodine. "I told you not to play in the street," his mother said, kissing him gently on the forehead. He angrily pushed her away—didn't she know how he hated the way iodine smelled, the way it stung? But she spilled the tiny bottle—it dripped down his face—onto his pillow. "Micky! Now look what you've made me do," she said crossly, but she wasn't sitting on the bed anymore. She was hovering above it, like a kite. He begged her to give him a clean pillow, but she wouldn't. She couldn't. She was gone.

He couldn't see the face of the girl standing at his bureau. Seaweed hung from her long hair—bubbles of bright green rockweed, and long brown, slippery kelp. Her dress looked like it was made of ragged ribbons of seaweed. Her feet were bare. He could hear her sobbing, but she wouldn't look at him. His bed was filled with seashells: clams and mussels, scallops and oysters, tiny periwinkles.

Claudia stood at the open door, the full moon behind her. "I lost my other earring," she said. "Help me find it, Mick." She held out her hand to him. A lone diamond earring lay in her open palm, its precious stones encrusted with barnacles.

He began to pull the kelp and rockweed from her hair, but no matter how much seaweed he pulled from it and threw to the floor, more slimy green took its place among her wet tangles. Soon the floor of his room was covered with sand and pebbles, shells and seaweed.

"I'm sorry I wore this dress." She frowned as she touched her hem. "Look, it's torn . . . "

A dark crimson stain was spreading over his white sheet. A book lay on the bed, but the stain was spreading over that, too—hiding the words he was reading. He took some turpentine and tried to wipe the alizarin crimson clean, but the stain kept spreading and spreading until he could no longer find the book.

He tried to draw her close to him, but her hand was cold and slippery, he couldn't hold on to it. He tried to grab her arm, but it, too, was slippery—it had silver scales. He slithered to the floor, and as he opened his mouth to cry out to her, it filled with sand.

Then he was in bed again, his sheets dry and clean. There was no trace of the alizarin stain, but the smell of seaweed and iodine still lingered.

She stood looking down at him, smiling and holding the bright moon in her hands. "Good-bye, Mick. I have to go now." She kissed him on the forehead, the way his mother had. Then she was gone. Only the moon remained behind, growing larger and brighter, filling his bed, his room. He tried to push it away, but he couldn't. It was steely cold and hard, its light was blinding him. . . .

Mick sat up in bed, wide awake. The door to his room was slightly ajar and the flashlight lay under the sheet, still lit. He saw a small smear of blood on his pillow from the cut on his cheek.

It was hot in the small room. He opened two windows for cross-ventilation and lay there, listening to the stillness of the hot summer night and recalling the dream.

In four years—not since she had died—it was the first time he had dreamed of Claudia. His tortured daylight visions of her were nothing like what he had experienced tonight, for unlike the hallucinations, the dream had left him feeling strangely refreshed and serene.

He knew she wouldn't come again. He touched his forehead where she had kissed him. It felt cool and somehow blessed. The cut on his cheek no longer caused him pain. He pulled off his jeans and shirt, and lay quietly in bed in his shorts. A soft breeze drifted through the room. Even the sea was silent.

Soon Mick thought he heard Crosby tiptoeing outside on the stairs, but when he opened the door and whistled softly for her, he knew she wasn't there. Soft mist hung over the house and garden, making the solitary light at the bend in the road shimmer.

As he stepped back inside, he noticed the bureau drawer was open. Something made him switch on the dim light on the dresser scarf. There was Claudia's photograph, smiling up at him—the same smile she had worn when she kissed him good-bye.

He took it out of the drawer. The frame was cool to his touch. He remembered the night his friend Leo had taken that photograph. He also remembered the enchanted morning a few days later, when he and Claudia had gone together to the Portobello Road at dawn where they found the antique silver frame she insisted had been designed by William Morris himself. Whether it was the work of the great Victorian or not didn't matter to Mick. It had simply been perfect for her portrait, and that was miracle enough.

"Good-bye, Claudia," he whispered. He kissed her image tenderly before putting the photograph into the inside pocket of his duffel and zipping it tight. Someday he would find a permanent place for it.

He switched off the light and got back into bed. The room was cooler now. He pulled the sheet up around his shoulders, lay on his side, and closed his eyes. As he sank into his pillow and drifted off to sleep, he remembered Leo had used his Hasselblad that night . . .

Mick woke early, for the morning sun rose like a ball of fire, quickly heating up the small room. He showered and dressed. When he looked out the window, he was surprised to see Penelope standing in the outside shower by the back door.

Her eyes were closed as she raised her face to the sparkling flow, like Artemis bathing in some sacred Arcadian spring. He stood looking down at her transfixed—watching her rinse salt and sand from her nude body before shampooing seawater from her hair. When she stepped out onto the sunlit grass, she dried her curls with a pink and white striped beach towel, then used her fingers as a comb. She wrapped the large towel around her before taking her wet bathing suit from where it dangled haphazardly over the shower door to hang it on the clothesline.

He went down the steps silently, and stood before her. She said nothing, but when she looked at him, the expression on her face was one of grave and tender trust and expectation. It was the same expression the young Helena Fourment wore in her husband's great wedding portrait of her.

I wish I could make a drawing of you the way you look right now, he thought, just as Rubens did his bride, so my loving you could also be remembered forever. For this is the way I will always see you, Penelope, as you are this morning.

"I didn't know you were back. I never heard you come in," he said at last.

"I flew over late last night, after the fog lifted. Then I walked home from the airport. I couldn't bear to spend another night in that place."

"I'm so glad you're here. It seemed like you were gone a long time."

"I was."

"Penelope?"

"Yes, Mick?"

"I dreamed of Claudia last night."

She slowly nodded in that sweet, solemn way she had, but said nothing.

"She came to say good-bye to me." Mick closed his eyes tight to lock in the tears he felt rising in them.

Penelope touched his cheek tenderly, and as she kissed him, the striped towel she was wearing fell to the ground.

He drew her to him and whispered, "Oh, God—I have missed you so!"

C H A P T E R

Sixteen

SUNLIGHT STREAMED IN on Penelope. She lay beside him on his bed, a glorious pink and gold vision of satisfied love. Her eyes were closed, but her full lips were slightly open, expectant, waiting. Mick watched her breasts move up and down as she breathed in slow and peaceful rhythm. He wondered if she was really sleeping or simply recalling her earlier joyous climax, savoring it in blissful solitude. He gently touched her lower lip and she smiled at his touch—a dreamer's smile. It seemed miraculous to Mick that he could feel aroused again so soon, but he was. He brushed his fingers across a rose-pink nipple.

"Come to me," she murmured, and drew him close.

Suddenly Mick heard the crunching sound of shoes walking on the remains of the gravel driveway right under the window. A woman's voice called, "Hel-lo-o-ooo! Yoo-hoo! Anybody home?"

"Oh, my God," he whispered. "Who the hell is that?"

Penelope opened her eyes wide. "I'm not expecting anyone."

"Yoo-hoo! Mrs. Winslow, are you there?" the voice called again, dispelling any doubts that she was in the right yard. Mick yanked on his shirt and peered surreptitiously from behind the curtain.

"It's some glamorous-looking blonde—sort of a Lauren Bacall type. From the way she's dressed, I'd say she's definitely not an islander. Sound like anyone you know?"

"No, it must be someone wanting to look at real estate. What will I do? I can't exactly go down like this, can I?" Penelope blushed. "I mean, I don't have any clothes."

He lay down beside her again. "Ignore her?" he whispered hopefully. "Just pray that she'll go away?" But he could still hear the insistent footsteps, and his magic moment passed.

"I'll get dressed and go down and see if I can stall her, at least get her onto the front porch. Then you'll be able to sneak in the back door, go upstairs and get dressed, then come down as though you just came up the road from collecting rent money from Meer, gathering mussels, or whatever. How's that?" Mick quickly pulled on his jeans and slipped into a pair of sandals as he spoke.

Penelope ran her fingers through his hair. "This morning you almost made me forget everything that's happening."

"Did I? I'm glad. You needed to forget for a while. Listen, Penelope, I was thinking about something earlier today . . . "

"Yes?"

"When all this is over, let's not rent the cottage again, okay? Instead, let's move into it. You, me—Sandy, too, whenever she's home from school. It's such a beautiful house. I'd like to see it full of our love. There's even a Steinway grand in it." He recalled that Penelope used to play the piano quite well. "Then I'll be able to use the studio just for work. I could use all that space for the new paintings I'm planning." The goddess pictures, he thought. The *Penelope* series. "What do you say?"

Her eyes filled with tears. "Ask me again, Mick. When all this is over."

"Because you're afraid you won't still love me when it is?" He smiled.

118

"No." She gazed at him solemnly. "I will love you forever. I told you that."

He went downstairs to where the stranger sat waiting on the back steps. "Good morning," he said. "Can I help you?"

"I'm looking for Mrs. Penelope Winslow. You don't happen to know where I'd find her, do you?" She had a socialite's accent—part elite finishing school, part theater—with no trace whatsoever of New England, or any other place that was real, for that matter.

"I saw her go down the road just a short while ago. I imagine she'll be back soon. In the meantime, why don't you make yourself comfortable on the front porch? My name's Mick Merisi, by the way. I'm Mrs. Winslow's tenant." He put out his hand to her.

"Marina Johnson." Mick noticed she was wearing Calèche. Claudia had a bottle of it, long ago.

Penelope soon joined them and introduced herself. "Have you come to look at island properties? I'm sorry, but I'm afraid I usually show them by appointment only." Her voice was courteous, but aloof and wary.

"No, that's not why I'm here." Marina shot a quick glance in Mick's direction. "Mrs. Winslow, I'd like to speak to you in private, if possible. It's about something rather important."

"Mr. Merisi's a good friend of mine. He's welcome to stay and hear anything you have to tell me."

The visitor fingered a pair of pendants she wore on a gold chain around her neck—a gold tennis racquet with a small diamond on the strings and the word "LOVE" shining next to it. She opened her purse, took out an official-looking laminated card bearing her photograph. "I've been retained by Attorney Winslow to research a certain confidential matter pertaining to his daughter, Cassandra."

"Ms. Johnson—"

"Mrs.," Marina corrected her.

Penelope frowned. "Sorry. Mrs. Johnson, are you telling me my ex-husband has hired you to investigate Sandy?"

"Yes."

"Without her knowledge?"

"That's been my understanding."

"But I just spoke with him last night. He never mentioned such an arrangement to me. What has he told you, exactly?" Mick detected a slight quaver in Penelope's voice.

"That she has recently confessed to a homicide. He has therefore retained me in order to rule out any possibility whatsoever that her confession is valid. He's already informed me what Cassandra has told him herself of the situation, which is, frankly, next to nothing."

Penelope's eyes were bright with anger. "Mrs. Johnson, please get this straight. I'm not going to let you start snooping through my daughter's things. She's not a criminal. She's just a young girl who's having some sort of a tragic breakdown. I don't know what possessed Chap to ask you to do this, but I'm asking you to leave my house, right now. Excuse me." She went inside, slamming the screen door after her.

Marina Johnson swept a lock of professionally streaked blond hair away from her cheekbone. A collection of gold bangle bracelets tinkled on her wrist. Her long and perfect nails were newly painted scarlet and a white silk blouse showed off a smooth, even tan. She made Mick think of what a fresh miracle of nature Penelope was—her full, round, perfect breasts, those delicate blue veins beneath the milk-white skin, the nipples like rosebuds, the way she quivered so exquisitely beneath his touch—

"Mr. Merisi?"

"Yes—sorry. What were you saying?"

"Heavens! I'd sure give more than a penny for *your* thoughts!" She gave him a coy sideways look from beneath her lashes, smiled a Cheshire Cat smile. "I was just about to say that I'll be happy to leave now, if that's what Mrs. Winslow really wants."

"It appears to be, doesn't it?"

"Too bad. She might have found some details of my investigation interesting." She pulled some car keys from her purse and smoothed her short, cream-colored linen skirt as she got up. "But

120

I guess I'll just tootle along now. *Ciao!* So awfully nice to have met you, Mr. Merisi. Please say good-bye to Mrs. Winslow for me." She smiled a perfunctory smile and sauntered down the hot and weedy country road on elegant Italian spectator pumps, then got into a black Saab convertible. She took a swig from a bottle of Evian before driving away.

"Jesus! Where'd he find her?" Mick muttered. His only knowledge of private detectives came from whatever he'd learned watching reruns of *The Rockford Files*.

He found Penelope on the phone in her office. "I don't know how you could do this without discussing it with me first," she was saying. "You always say one thing, then go and do something entirely different." She paused. "Hiring that woman is what I mean, Chap—" Mick heard his voice loudly interrupt, but couldn't make out what Chap said. "I don't care whether you say she's the best in the business or not, or whether you've successfully worked with her on lots of divorce and missing heirs cases. That's neither here nor there." Penelope's voice dropped sadly. "It almost sounds as though you think Sandy's guilty. And if you do, I don't think we have anything more to discuss. Good-bye, Chap." She hung up the phone, put her head in her hands, and began to sob.

"Penelope," said Mick, "will you listen to me, please, darling?" He had to be tactful, he knew, for he was aware that his own role in trying to find out what happened wasn't, after all, that different from Marina Johnson's. At least, he suspected it wouldn't seem so to an outside observer—or to Chap Winslow, either.

She wouldn't look at him, just went on sobbing into her hands.

"Okay, I need to look through some of Sandy's things—right now. But I won't do it, not if you don't want me to."

"I *do* want you to." She flung her arms around him and cried, "Mick, Chap never told me he was planning to send this woman on her trail. Why didn't he? I thought the two of us were going to cooperate in trying to help her!"

"Penelope, it doesn't matter now whether he consulted you or not. I think Chap probably hired this detective to uncover some-thing Sandy's trying desperately to hide."

"He thinks she did it," Penelope said glumly.

"I know she didn't do it, but I also know she's hiding some-thing. And at some point she's going to have to tell someone what it is and why." He kissed her. "I love you so," he whispered, then went upstairs to Sandy's room.

He had no trouble locating her large black portfolio, for it lay on the floor under her bed. He had kept his in the same place when he was a student. When Mick opened it, he went through endless composition studies on large sheets of newsprint: cones, cylinders, and balls rendered in grimy charcoal. Soon he came to her life studies. Sandy had the ability to create a recognizable like-ness, a gift that invariably impressed those who were not artists, and that artists themselves knew to be insignificant. He skipped quickly over the male nudes, and didn't find the girl among the female ones.

Then he found one lone page ripped from a spiral-bound sketchbook. The full-face pencil portrait was poorly composed, with a lifeless, tentative line, and numerous erasures. Like every other drawing in the portfolio, this one was neatly signed "Cas-sandra Winslow."

Sandy had captured the girl's features all right—her perfect oval face, her long neck, the bee-stung upper lip, those almond-shaped Botticelli eyes with their blank and innocent-seeming gaze.

Mick was about to close the portfolio, when he saw a manila envelope lying between some still-life studies he'd overlooked. He opened it and pulled out a photograph identical to the exhibition-quality 8 × 10 print Evgeny Otkresta had added to his own work-in-progress. Mick glanced at it quickly, then put it back in the envelope, along with Sandy's drawing. He had what he wanted, now.

He slid the portfolio back under the bed, but kept the manila envelope.

Penelope was still at her desk, doodling aimlessly on a memo pad, her cheeks stained with tears. "Did you find anything?"

Mick shrugged. "Not really. I need some more time. Listen"—he tried to sound both confident and casual—"do you think you could arrange it somehow that I can see Sandy—that I can talk to her?"

"You could go with me when I visit next time."

"No," Mick said. "I mean alone, without you."

Penelope looked at him with terror in her eyes. "You think she did it, too, don't you, Mick? Just the way Chap does?"

"No, I don't. But I think she might know who did, and why. I hope that when she hears Chap's hired a detective, she'll decide to talk to me, before Mrs. Johnson finds out more than Sandy wants her to know. Anyway, that's what I want to try to persuade her to do."

She nodded. Tears welled up in her eyes again and Mick drew her to him.

"I'll try to arrange it," she said after a moment. "Chap must know all about these legal procedures, but I hope I won't have to ask him to help me." She lay her head against Mick's chest.

"Penelope? Don't be afraid to ask him for help if you have to. I mean—hell—he's her father. I'm sure he wants to help her as much as you do."

"I know, Mick, I know." She took a deep breath, then dried her eyes. "I'll have to go over and talk to someone in charge. Everything has to be done by filling out ten thousand forms, I suppose." She looked at the small digital clock on her desk. "Maybe I can still get there in time, if I take a plane."

She pulled an airline schedule from the top drawer and studied it. "There's a flight in twenty minutes. Would you mind driving me to the airport, Mick?"

Seventeen

PALMER'S BOATYARD WAS closed.

"Damn it!" Mick exclaimed in frustration. He needed details about the morning Evgeny Otkresta had been in there buying the kite.

He looked at his watch. He had more than three hours to kill before Penelope would telephone him at the house, letting him know what arrangement, if any, she'd been able to make for him to visit Sandy.

He decided to stop in at Ry Pinkham's General Store and pin a note on the community bulletin board saying Crosby was missing. He offered a twenty-five-dollar reward, feeling certain that would assure all the island children kept a sharp lookout for her.

Stopping a few moments to pass the time of day with the storekeeper might also give him some information, useless or otherwise, for everyone on the island came through there eventually.

"Been to the art gallery yet?" Ry asked.

"No. I didn't know there was one. Is that something new?"

"Yep. Didn't used to be here, but 'tis now. Nice fellow who runs it, too. Foreign, but that's all right by me. Yep, he just finished fixing up the old bike rental shop. Should be good for the summer folks."

Mick turned the corner and went down a short dirt road. He dodged a barefoot, sunburned young woman teetering precariously through the road's many ruts and pebbles on a rusty bicycle. She wore a sacklike dress of some handwoven cloth that defied anyone to guess what color it was meant to be. She also looked alarmingly close to giving birth. Besides the child she carried in her womb, another large, bovine one energetically sucked a pacifier as he or she rode in a bicycle seat behind the woman. She waved a smiling greeting as she passed Mick, making him certain she was either a summer visitor or some newcomer to the island. Natives were seldom that friendly.

A stocky man with a bushy red beard was up on a ladder in front of the old bicycle rental shop. He wore a shirt of a fabric identical to the woman's dress and was hanging a sign over the entrance that said: "Dorf's Wharf."

"Hello," Mick called up. "Is this the art gallery?"

"Yes." The man climbed down from the ladder and shook Mick's hand. "I'm Alain Dorfer. Please, won't you come in?"

His Teutonic appearance and German-sounding last name, combined with a strong French accent and first name, made Mick guess him to be Alsatian.

Dorfer opened the door and proudly gestured for Mick to precede him. The old building and the rickety dock behind it had been transformed into a bright, white, cheerful space. Crudely shaped raku pots with none of the vital energy and elegance of their Japanese originals stood on shelves and pedestals placed here and there around the large room.

"How'd you happen to come out to Dutchman's Island?" Mick asked, as he looked around at the ceramics.

"My wife inherited some property here—the original Bingham farmhouse. We're hoping we can survive through the winter. It will be a wonderful place to raise a family, no?"

"I should imagine so. I know the house well. It's a beautiful spot—fabulous views."

"Ah, yes!" Alain Dorfer beamed. "We were living in Vermont, but one day we came over here to look at the property, to decide whether to sell it or not. But as soon as we saw Dutchman's Island, we immediately fell in love with the place."

"That's easy to do," said Mick.

"I think our gallery will go over quite well. Besides works of art we are also planning to sell organic baked goods, handwoven cloth, homespun wool from our sheep, herbs and island honey. Perhaps we will serve coffee, too. Yes." He tenderly stroked his beard. "I really think we will do well. The summer tourists are beginning to come, and I have heard there is considerable local talent on the island."

"Are you going to be open awhile?" Mick asked. "There's something—someone's work—I'd like to show you, if you have a minute."

"By all means."

Mick ran to his van, took the manila envelope from the seat, and promptly returned to the gallery. "I wonder if you're familiar with this person's work?" He handed Dorfer the photograph he had taken from Sandy's portfolio that morning.

"But this is extraordinary! Truly extraordinary!" Dorfer began searching around in a pile of papers that lay on the unpainted sawhorses and plywood plank serving as his desk. He soon pulled a similar manila envelope from under an electrician's bill. A duplicate of the picture Mick held in his hand was inside, along with two others he hadn't yet seen.

In the first, the girl was wearing a white wimple and long velvet dress of medieval design. She held up the hem of her skirt over a belly as swollen as that of Dorfer's wife, while demurely holding the hand of a young man of quite spectacular beauty, who was garbed in a fur-trimmed velvet coat and large hat. The two of them were posing as the man and wife in van Eyck's famous Arnolfini marriage portrait. The girl knew her art history, Mick decided. But in the round mirror on the back wall—that spot where the self-portrait of the painter usually lurked to tantalize posterity—Mick saw a pale and grinning skull. Instead of the merry little terrier who normally stood in the foreground of the painting, there was a montaged tabloid image of a snarling pit bull champing at a disembodied, bleeding human hand.

The third photograph was a full frontal nude of the girl stretched out alone on a divan. Although she wore a ponderous black wig and a coy smirk, posing as Goya's *Naked Maja*, she still couldn't disguise her distinctive face and body.

"She was in here—oh, perhaps a week or so ago," Dorfer said. "I found her work somewhat interesting, so I asked if she had enough pieces for a one-man show. She said yes, she definitely did. One thing was most peculiar, however." He frowned, appearing puzzled.

"Yes?"

"She insisted she would have to hang the show herself, with no assistance from me at all. And that she *had* to hang it alone the day of the opening. I was also not to see any work in advance. It was an unusual request, but since she agreed to bear all the costs of the exhibit, I saw no reason not to agree to her terms."

"When will the show be?"

"That's just it—I don't know, now. She left these with me," he pointed to the photographs, "said she'd be back in a day or so, but she has never returned."

Mick studied the pictures. He was reminded of work by another artist whose art consisted of eerie photographs she took of herself posing as someone else—someone famous. He knew from experience what a good job art schools did at turning out clones of last year's trendiest gallery stars. He turned the pictures over, expecting perhaps to find a pretentious title for each one written on the back, but the white photographic paper was blank. Even the usual credit and phone number was missing, but that didn't surprise him.

"She's quite influenced by Cindy Sherman, wouldn't you say?"

"That's her name—Cindy Sherman!" Dorfer exclaimed. "I had forgotten it. So you *have* heard of her? She is well known?"

"Very."

It looked like the girl traveled under more than one alias, using the names of other female artists than Vanessa Bell. Mick felt he wouldn't be surprised to trace her as Georgia O'Keeffe, Mary Cassatt, Gwen John, or whoever her whimsy decided she'd be for that day, week, or year. A strange young woman—one he found difficult, if not impossible, to connect with wholesome and unsophisticated Cassandra Winslow.

Mick sensed Alain Dorfer hadn't heard about the body on Wrecker's Point yet. Not that there was any reason for him to connect that death with the artist he'd met. And it was quite possible that as a newcomer to the island, he had no acquaintances who might have told him of it.

Mick decided it was best to keep a low profile—not to let it get around that he was investigating on his own—so he said nothing. He didn't tell the gallery owner that the young woman who called herself Cindy Sherman would never return to hang her show on his newly painted white walls.

He handed Dorfer his photographs. "There's another painter out here who I understand is also an up-and-coming superstar— a young Russian émigré named Evgeny Otkresta."

"Hair bleached white? All black glitzy clothes? Very little English?"

"That sounds like him. Has he been in here?"

"He came with her, but he never mentioned to me that he was also an artist."

"Oh, yes, he is. If he does happen to come around again, could you please give me a call? My name's Mick, by the way." He jotted down Penelope's telephone number. "You can reach me here. And good luck with the show."

"Thank you. You'll be sure and come to the opening, won't you?"

"I'll try."

As soon as Mick pulled into the driveway, he felt a strong impulse to return to the boathouse where Claudia stored *Felicity*.

He didn't know why. He suspected that he irrationally hoped Claudia's serene and confident ability to navigate stormy waters might guide him to where he'd understand the reason why the picture the dead girl had left with Dorfer seemed the most important discovery he had made up to now.

Mick had no idea why he felt it was. After all, it wasn't the least bit strange that an aspiring and ambitious artist would show her work to the only dealer on the island. He might have done the same thing once. And given the pastiche starring herself he had earlier found on Evgeny Otkresta's collage, the dead girl's version of van Eyck's Arnolfini marriage portrait was a predictable stylistic statement.

As he walked toward the boathouse Mick wondered if he hadn't been mistaken about the vision he'd had of Claudia. He felt now he needed to be near her again—near the boat she had loved. Perhaps she hadn't come that night to say good-bye after all.

For a moment he feared that perhaps Claudia would always be drawing him to her, always asserting her presence into his love for Penelope.

No. He wasn't going to let that happen. Never again.

He was just about to return to the room over Penelope's garage when he noticed the padlock on the boathouse door had been removed.

He ran to the boathouse and pushed hard against the door, but it didn't open.

It must be locked from the inside. But why? he wondered.

He remembered there was one window in the back of the shed, but when he went around the building, he saw that the rugosa roses that normally grew below the window had grown high and covered it.

Mick took out his pocket knife and cut away some of the rose canes. The window was so dirty it was difficult to see anything. He rubbed it with his shirt. Behind the spiderweb that filled one inside corner of the window he could see a sketch pad and felt-tip pen lying on the tarpaulin covering *Felicity*.

Then he saw. Crosby lying on her side in a corner by the door, her front paws stretched out stiffly in front of her. Mick couldn't see if her eyes were open. He didn't want to know if they were or not, because the small, thin cat looked quite dead.

From under the shrouded hull of the boat he saw a bare arm reaching toward her. It was covered with bruises. Mick knocked loudly against the windowpane, but the hand didn't move.

Mick ran toward the house to telephone the police.

Minutes later, the car arrived. A dusty and antiquated station wagon followed, bearing a sign on its door: EMERGENCY MEDICAL SERVICE, DUTCHMAN'S ISLAND.

The new cop was small and dark. George emerged from the station wagon and trotted across the lawn beside her.

"Mr. Merisi? I'm Sergeant Diaz," she said. "Is this the building?" She pointed to the shed.

A crowbar and hatchet in the trunk of the police car enabled George to break down the door quickly. Once again, Mick heard the fractured, bulletlike static sounds of the police radio—all confusion—numbers, codes, a language he didn't comprehend.

Sergeant Diaz knelt beside the arm, while George yanked the tarpaulin away from where it hid the rest of the body. Numerous drawings of cats, impatiently ripped from a sketchbook, littered the floor. A hypodermic needle lay next to Evgeny Otkresta.

"What do you think, Rosie?" George said. "Looks like he OD'd, doesn't it? Shit, it's awful hot in here! Stinks like hell—"

Mick stepped away from the shed to be sick.

CHAPTER

Eighteen

"WHY DON'T YOU mind your own business?" Sandy said petulantly. "I don't need your help, or anyone's else's."

Mick glanced over at the guard, then at his watch. He was getting nowhere, and time was running out.

"I had an interesting telephone conversation this morning with the dean of students at Arts and Crafts," he said. "Matter of fact, she's an old classmate of mine."

He glimpsed a flash of terror in Sandy's face, but it quickly vanished and the former sullenness replaced it.

"Aren't you curious about what we discussed?" Mick asked.

"No! Not at all." She turned her head, avoiding his steady gaze.

"She told me that you're going to get an incomplete in all your courses for the last semester because you haven't attended them for the last two and a half months."

"Oh, she's crazy. Most of the time those jerks don't even take attendance," Sandy mumbled.

Mick sighed. "No, she's not crazy, Sandy. And have you forgotten that I used to be one of those jerks? They take attendance."

"Just because you—"

"Did your father know you weren't there?" Mick interrupted her.

She shook her head.

"Your mother sure as hell didn't either. Where have you been staying?"

She didn't answer.

"I don't believe you killed that girl, but I'm sure you knew her. In fact, I found a drawing of her in your portfolio."

"What were you doing looking at my portfolio? You were snooping around in my room?" she demanded angrily.

"Yes. I found it under the bed—exactly where I used to keep mine. Who is she?"

"Who gave you permission to go looking through my private things when I wasn't there?" She glared at him. "Was it Mom?"

"Goddamn it, Sandy, grow up for Christ's sake!" Mick exclaimed. "Yeah, of course it was your mother. She loves you. She's trying to help you. So am I."

"Then you can go away and leave me alone. Tell Mom I'm not worth her worrying about," Sandy whispered, her voice breaking.

"Listen, Sandy," Mick said. "Did you know that your father has hired a private detective to find out what's really going on— to uncover why you've put yourself in this damned place?"

Mick knew he'd reached Sandy with this news. "Oh, my God!" she wailed, hiding her face in her hands.

"That's why I'm hoping you'll tell me what happened—what really happened—I mean," Mick persisted. "You have to admit it would be better if you told me the truth before she finds out what it is you're trying to hide, whom you're trying to cover up for."

It appeared Sandy had forgotten for the moment to deny that she was hiding anything, cover up for anyone. Instead she let down her guard and ingenuously asked, "She? Who's she?"

"The detective your father has retained. A woman named Marina Johnson," Mick said wearily.

Sandy wiped her eyes and stared at Mick. "Mrs. Johnson?

132

She's a private detective?" she asked with obvious amazement.

"I assume you know her."

"Well, sort of." She pushed a stray strand of hair away from her cheek. "She's Dad's doubles partner at the tennis club. How weird! Mrs. Johnson's a real detective?" Sandy repeated in disbelief.

"So she says. And I believe her. She has a license; I saw it. Your mother's pretty damned angry that she's snooping around in your life. So I told her I'd try to find out what was going on before Mrs. Johnson did." He shrugged. "Of course, I'll admit I'm at a considerable disadvantage in this race. After all, she's a pro and I'm sure as hell not."

Sandy crossed her arms, puffed her cheeks, and let out her breath loudly. She narrowed her eyes and scrutinized Mick. Mick no longer saw the frightened, guileless child he had faced moments before. Now her look was adult, hard, searching, and wary. He said nothing, but waited for her to speak.

"Why are you involved in this anyway, Mr. Merisi?" she asked quietly, at last. "You should be relieved that the police have got me. Now they won't suspect you of killing her, will they?" She made an attempt at a sardonic smile. "After all, you found her body."

"Oh, Christ! Come off it! When you heard the news down at the harbor, Sandy—remember how you came running to tell your mother about it?"

"I don't remember," she said.

"Well, I do. You sure didn't act like someone who'd just killed someone. You said old Tom Girtin did it, remember?"

She shrugged.

"Anyway, I'm not at all sure the police don't suspect me," Mick continued. "Not sure at all. But that's not why I'm involved, Sandy, believe me." He sighed and ran his fingers through his hair.

This sure as hell wasn't the right time to tell Cassandra Winslow that he'd fallen in love with her mother, and she with him.

"Then go away," Sandy implored. "Please, Mr. Merisi—just go away."

"No. Sorry, but you're stuck with me," Mick replied. "Sandy, Claudia loved you very much. I wouldn't be doing justice to her memory if I didn't try to stop you from doing this crazy thing."

Yes—that was part of the truth, Mick told himself. But his own truth was, just as he suspected Sandy's of being, considerably more complicated than he revealed.

"Well, I wouldn't bother anymore, if I were you," she said scornfully.

Mick ignored what she had said. "I don't believe for one minute that you killed that girl, Sandy. I thought I knew who did, and I've been trying on my own to track him down. Now I may never find out if he did or not, because he's dead."

Again the look of terror returned. "Who? Who's dead?"

"Evgeny Otkresta. It looks like a drug overdose."

"She probably sold them to him." Sandy appeared relieved when she said this.

"So she was a drug dealer?"

"Among other things."

"Sandy, I know you're hiding something—"

She tried to protest, but Mick continued. "I found a drawing of her in your portfolio. I know"—he held up his hand—"don't look at me like that. I don't like snooping, either. But before long, Mrs. Johnson's going to find out what it is you're hiding. As soon as she does, she'll be obligated to let your father know, since he's paying her to do just that." He spoke gently now. "Wouldn't you rather tell me, Sandy, before she does that? I won't repeat anything you say to anyone."

Tears ran down her cheeks. "Do you mean that? Can I really trust you?" Her expression was pleading.

"Yes."

"You promise?"

"I promise. You knew her well, didn't you?"

She nodded sadly.

"I think you were close friends once, but all that changed—for some reason."

Again she nodded. "I hated her more than I thought it was possible to hate anyone."

"Tell me something."

"What?"

"First, I want you to promise you'll tell the truth."

She hesitated before mumbling, "I promise."

"Did you kill her?"

To Mick's surprise, she answered promptly, her eyes flashing. "No, but I'm glad she's dead! And I could have killed her—I hated her so. I think someone killed her because she deserved it."

"Such as Evgeny Otkresta?"

"It wasn't him," she whispered.

"Who, then?"

She looked away.

"Come on, Sandy, tell me who," Mick said.

She remained silent.

Mick decided to try another tack. "Did you write the note the police found on her?"

"Yes."

He waited for her to tell her story. He believed she wanted to—needed to. But Sandy hid her face in her hands, the way he had seen Penelope do, and her body soon shook with sobs.

Mick let her cry until she looked up at him and said again, "Do you mean it? Can I really trust you? Trust you not to tell *anyone* in the world what I tell you—not the police, not Mrs. Johnson, not Mom or Dad, not anyone?"

"You can. I promise."

"Even if you think they should know—for my own good?"

"Even then. I might hope you'd tell someone what's happened, but I won't presume to do it for you. I give you my solemn word on that."

She took a deep breath. "Her name wasn't Vanessa Bell. It was Sabrina Ferris."

"No relation to Joanna Ferris, by any chance?"

She nodded. "Her mom. Mrs. Moneybags."

Mick whistled softly. When the police found out who their Jane Doe was, it was going to be big news. Very big news.

Joanna Ferris was rich, socially prominent, and well known for the way she spread her vast fortune generously around museums, ballet companies, theaters—any other hungry cultural organization. Yes, he knew her name well, as did anyone who tried to earn a living in the arts.

"What the hell did Sabrina Ferris do to make you write that note?" he asked. "It must have been something pretty bad."

She didn't answer.

"Did she come to Dutchman's Island because of you?"

"She had no other reason to. She'd never heard of the place until she met me."

"But what did she do? You still haven't told me."

Sandy looked at him steadily. "I guess you'd say she ruined my life, that's all. For the fun of it—for the same reason she did every other cruel and evil thing she dreamed up. And she wanted to ruin everyone else's—everyone I love, at least. Everyone who loves me." She fidgeted with the hem on her skirt and her lower lip trembled.

Mick felt like a hunter stalking his prey. But he saw he was finally reaching her, and before his visit was over, might understand what motivated Sandy in the bizarre, self-destructive thing she had elected to do. "How did she do that, Sandy?"

She didn't answer.

"How come she used an alias? What was she hiding?"

"I don't know. Maybe something—maybe nothing. Personally, I think she did it simply because she *could*. She had fake driver's licenses, fake credit cards, even a fake passport, all in different names. But I don't know why. She thought it was fun to trick people." Sandy shook her head sadly. "When I first met her, I thought it was cool—the way I thought everything about her was cool."

It wasn't difficult for Mick to understand how a girl like Sabrina Ferris, with the glamour that came with beauty and great wealth, could easily cast a spell, malevolent or otherwise, over someone with Cassandra Winslow's insular and bucolic upbringing.

"As soon as I got to Arts and Crafts, I knew I didn't belong there," Sandy said glumly. "Sabrina was probably the best of the best. I wasn't in her league at all. It seemed as though the best of the best in that place meant the weirdest of the weird. Do you know what I mean?"

"All too well," Mick said.

She continued, "Not just at photography, either. Sabrina was good at drawing, painting, sculpture, design—the works. She transferred to Arts and Crafts last year as a sophomore to major in photography." Sandy closed her eyes, a look of pain on her face. "She always carried that Hasselblad wherever she went. I knew it had to be her when you mentioned the camera. No one else had one. I should have known how creepy she was when I saw the pictures she'd taken of herself in a coffin. I couldn't believe she'd paid all this money to an undertaker so she could get dressed up and go lie in a fancy satin-lined coffin! I thought the pictures were gruesome, but the faculty exhibition committee chose to hang them in the cafeteria, so I knew *they* thought they were good. I just figured I didn't know what art was."

"How the hell did you two happen to become friends? It doesn't sound as though you had much in common."

"Just because she lived next door to me on my dorm. No, that's not true. She really seemed to *want* to be best friends with me. She singled me out. You can't imagine how nice she could seem, when she wanted to." Sandy appeared embarrassed by what she was about to say. "I shouldn't say this, but before I got to know her, she reminded me of someone."

"Claudia?"

"Yes." She opened her eyes wide. "How did you guess I was going to say that?"

"Because I thought the same thing, at first."

When he said that, Mick knew he had made a contract with Sandy—that now they spoke the same language.

"Then you can imagine how easy it was to like her. I liked the way she called me Cassandra, the way Claudia always did. I liked how she told me everyone thought we looked like sisters. I knew it wasn't true—she was so gorgeous! But something was similar, I guess." She bit her lower lip.

Mick looked at her. She resembled her father more than her mother. He saw a pleasant, wholesome-looking girl with none of Penelope's peaches-and-cream, full-blown beauty. Still, Sandy had clear, bronze, silky skin, long dark lashes on her gray eyes, and a wide and ready smile. Yes, she had the potential of being damned attractive, with her long, slender limbs, swan neck, and graceful carriage. There was definitely something about her that could be considered at least superficially to resemble the breathtaking creature he'd seen rising from the sea that night.

"Stupid me! I liked it when she borrowed things like my camera strap. I mean, everything she had was expensive, but she still wanted my crummy things. Why, I don't know." She paused. "One day, Sabrina said she wanted to show me some photographs she'd just developed. She wanted my opinion as to whether they'd be good pieces to put in the first semester student show." Sandy shook her head in disbelief. "That's when I found out how cruel she could be."

"How?"

"Well, everyone in his class knew that one of our teachers—Mr. Mann—was crazy about his graduate assistant, even though he was married. Somehow, Sabrina had managed to take pictures of him with her. They were off in some dunes—a very private place where they were probably sure they were alone. You'd never believe *anyone* could take pictures like that! That's when she told me how she'd been following people ever since she was a little kid, spying on them. I told her she couldn't possibly put those pictures in the show. I mean, Mr. Mann was a nice guy—"

"Did she exhibit them?" Mick saw himself gazing at Sabrina Ferris in the moonlight, with the strobe on the Hasselblad shooting off. What irony that she had called him a voyeur.

"No. She said she'd do whatever I told her to. The funny thing was, she was his favorite student. I don't mean because she was beautiful, or because her mother was a big shot, either. No, Mr. Mann thought the world of Sabrina because she was so talented. I didn't understand how she could do that to anyone, least of all someone who cared about her."

"You haven't told me anything so far, have you, Sandy? Everything you've said concerns someone else. What did she do to *you*—Cassandra Winslow—to make you write a note saying you could kill her? That's pretty strong stuff."

Sandy closed her eyes. Mick watched her lips move silently as though she were praying. Soon she took a deep breath and said tonelessly, "One weekend after Christmas break, she invited me to go to New York with her. We drove down in my car." She clenched her fists and shut her eyes again. "Don't make me tell you, please don't—" she begged.

"Why did you decide to plead guilty to killing her?" he asked, patiently.

"I remember Dad once talking about plea bargaining, how it kept things from coming out in a trial. Your lawyer just tells the judge you did it, and then he figures out what your sentence will be. That's it."

"I assume you have a lawyer?"

"Yes."

"And you've talked with him, and told him why you want to do this?"

"No. I told him I *did* do it, but I'm not sure he believes me."

"Suppose he won't go along with your scheme?"

"Then I'll get another lawyer. One who will!" she whispered fiercely. The guard looked over at her.

"Oh, God! I'm so confused," she said, cradling her head in her arms on the table. "I know you're right—Mrs. Johnson's going to find out eventually, anyway. And of course she'll tell Dad what happened, and he'll tell Mom. And maybe, since Mrs. Johnson's a detective—God, I still can't believe that—she'll find out who *did* do it, and tell the police."

"That's what you're really afraid of, isn't it?"

She nodded.

"Who are you protecting? Who do you think did it?"

"No one." The sullen look returned to her face and she answered flippantly, "I mean, how should I know?"

"Okay, we'll get back to that later," Mick said. "Tell me about the weekend in New York."

She nodded like an obedient child. He had already observed she had the mercurial mood changes of a deeply troubled person—the sort of changes he himself had felt too often in the past four years.

"She wanted me to wear her clothes and jewelry, so I did—all black and silver, like poor Evgeny. She kept saying how much I looked like her. Then, this was weird . . . " Sandy paused.

"What was?"

"Well, she said I looked exactly like she would look, *if she was good.* I didn't understand what she was talking about. I mean, I thought she was kidding about the whole dressing alike thing, the way I was. But I soon realized she was deadly serious—the way she kept saying how she wanted everyone who saw us to think we were twins. It began to scare me, although I didn't let her know that. But when we drove down to New York, I forgot my uneasy feelings because it was so exciting, I'd never been there before. A guy she knew named Dennis had a loft in SoHo. We were planning to stay with him. There was something about him I didn't like. Something creepy . . . "

I wonder if he was the guy in the Arnolfini marriage portrait? Mick thought. A fellow narcissist.

"The three of us went to some galleries in SoHo. Then we bought bread, cheese, a jug of wine, and went back to his loft and listened to music. After a while, Sabrina started asking him if he didn't think I looked like her. Finally he said yes, but it sounded to me as though he just said it to shut her up. We ate supper, and she kept giving him these coy looks and he would grin, as though they shared some secret I wasn't in on." She pressed her fingers against her temples, as though she felt pain there. "Something was

140

in that wine or cheese, because suddenly I went crazy—I mean, really crazy! The walls were all closing in on me, I wanted to go out the window. I thought I could fly, but I was terrified. I could hear voices jabbering at me, and I was screaming for them to be quiet—to go away. But they wouldn't."

"Sounds like acid," Mick murmured.

Sandy nodded. "Probably. I had guessed she sold drugs at school, but I knew she never took them herself. I don't think any of whatever it was was in their food, just mine. Pretty soon he and Sabrina were grabbing my arms, because I was trying to run away—crying and yelling. Finally she got me to swallow some pill. I don't know what it was but it calmed me down—fast. Too fast. I felt like I was melting, sinking into the floor, like the Wicked Witch of the West. I was dizzy, so she helped me to bed. I felt myself sinking into the mattress, then floating."

She shuddered. "I thought I fell asleep and dreamed he and Sabrina were kissing, and she took his shirt off. Suddenly she pointed to me and said 'Look, Dennis! Isn't she lovely? So sweet! So innocent!' He laughed—a crazy laugh—and pulled the covers off me. I knew then I wasn't dreaming. I tried to get away from him, but I couldn't. A bright light flashed, but I thought it was still whatever garbage I'd taken. He pushed me down, and I screamed and begged Sabrina to tell him to stop, but she . . . " Sandy hid her face and began to rock back and forth, moaning with grief.

"Oh Jesus!" Mick said. "I'm sorry. Oh God! I'm sorry." He reached for her hand and held it, stroked it gently.

"I'm so ashamed," she whispered.

He tried to find words to console her, but none came. He was too shocked.

"Then the two of them just left, went out on the town somewhere, cool as can be—as though nothing had happened. As soon as they were gone, I somehow got myself out of there, found my car, and drove back to school alone. I don't know why I wasn't killed. I was still spaced out, and it had started to snow. The roads were slippery. But I made it somehow—I guess because I didn't care whether I did or not. When Sabrina came back Monday, I

avoided her, and she did me. But I couldn't concentrate on anything, couldn't finish assignments. I couldn't sleep—couldn't stop
thinking about what happened. I felt so ashamed. . . .

"Anyway, when spring came, Johnny Selcott drove over to see
me one day. I was surprised, because I never knew him that well
on the island. But I was glad he did, because being with him was
so wonderful—like the fresh, clean air at home. It seemed as
though I could almost pretend none of that stuff ever happened.
I didn't say no to Johnny when—you know—" She looked shyly
at Mick, and for a moment she was beautiful. "He told me how
he was glad I was the first girl he'd made love to. He told me he'd
loved me ever since I was in kindergarten and he was in second
grade, that even back then he wanted to marry me when we both
grew up." A look of tender reminiscence crossed her face. "Can
you imagine that?"

Mick smiled. "Of course I can. It's easy to imagine someone
loving you that much."

"I kept thinking, here was the sweetest person in the world who
loved *me*. I knew it would kill him if he ever found out what happened, so I decided I'd never tell him. Never! But one day Sabrina came to my room, acted real friendly, and started talking
about how she'd noticed I had a boyfriend. I acted real cold, hoping she'd get the hint and get out of there, but she didn't go. Instead, she said how good-looking Johnny was—which is true. Before long, she got to the point and told me that since she'd shared
her lover with me, it was only fair that now I should share *mine*
with her. Because, weren't we sisters? I felt sick. At that moment
I understood how everything that happened that terrible weekend had been planned by her. When I asked her if I'd guessed
right, she just smiled and said, 'Why, Cassandra, you're not so
dumb after all, are you? Didn't you know I was the dark side of
the moon?' I can still hear her voice"—Sandy gazed at Mick with
the deepest sadness he had ever seen—"I wanted to kill her. I hit
her, and I *could* have killed her then, I know that. Now I wish I
had! But she didn't care that I hit her. She just stood there smirking, almost as though she wanted me to hurt her."

Mick recalled Vinnie telling him of the girl's identical response to Trudy's slap.

"She asked if I didn't want to see the pictures she'd taken that night in New York. . . . " A look of wild despair crossed Sandy's face. "When she showed them to me, I freaked out! I knew that if someone didn't know the whole story—about the drugs and everything—they might think from the pictures it was something I wanted. I mean, Sabrina was an artist! She was always in control of those disgusting pictures she took, she could distort things any way she wanted. I grabbed it and tore it up in little pieces, but she reminded me she still had the negative. 'I think Johnny Selcott would enjoy seeing it, don't you?' she said sweetly. Then I was really scared, because I'd never told her his name, and no one at school knew who he was. I didn't have any friends there."

"So you think she found it out from spying around the college?"

"Yes. She must have. She also said she thought my parents would like to know what I did while I was away at school." Sandy spoke without expression, as though she were reciting lines of a play she'd memorized, although she didn't yet comprehend their meaning.

"But she never showed it to anyone, did she?"

"I don't know. I didn't wait around to find out. That night I called Johnny at State U. and asked if he could find a place for me to stay. He had some friends who were sharing a house off-campus, so I moved in with them. He didn't ask why, or what happened, but to be on the safe side, I told him I was flunking out and didn't want Mom to know. He seemed to believe me. I got a part-time job in a supermarket to pay my share of the food and rent, and drove over to Arts and Crafts as often as I could to pick up my messages—which were always from Mom or Dad," she added poignantly.

She clasped her hands together until her knuckles were white. "Now I think Sabrina told Johnny about everything when she came to the island." She took a deep breath and continued speaking. "It wasn't Evgeny Otkresta you saw on the beach that night.

It couldn't have been, because he was at Vinnie's. I was there—remember? I saw him sitting alone at the bar."

"What are you telling me, Sandy?"

"Just that when I first saw him down at the harbor with Miss Glass, I noticed right away he was built sort of like Johnny—walks like him, too. And Johnny's got such light blond hair, they might look alike—from a distance at night, anyway. To someone who didn't really know either of them . . . " She paused, as more tears flowed down her cheeks. "Johnny said she had stopped at the boatyard Tuesday morning and told him she was a friend of mine from Arts and Crafts. She asked if he'd meet her on the beach that night, because she had something important to discuss with him—she was very worried about me. What a two-faced bitch!" Sandy spat out the words. "When I asked him what she said, he wouldn't tell me, said he didn't want to talk about it. The worst part was, he seemed angry at me, too. That's what makes me think she told him what happened."

"Had she ever hinted she'd be coming out to the island to look you up—to blackmail you?"

"No. In fact, she had even told me—long ago, when we were still friends—she was supposed to go sailing in Greece with her mother on someone's yacht all summer. They were going to leave as soon as school was out. Boy, I couldn't wait for that day to come! Then she'd be far away, probably find some other unsuspecting idiot to play her sick games, and forget all about me—and Johnny. I thought I'd never see her again." Color drained from her face. "When those two policemen came to the house to ask me some questions, I told them I did it."

"You confessed because you thought Johnny did it?" Mick asked incredulously.

"Yes."

"But he didn't have any motive for killing her, Sandy. I mean, why the hell would he?"

Sandy didn't answer. She didn't need to. The grief and shame Mick saw in her eyes spoke for her.

"Just because you thought Sabrina had told him what happened?"

She nodded.

"No! Christ—there's got to be something more than that," Mick exclaimed. "What else makes you so sure he did it, Sandy?"

She closed her eyes to keep back the tears. She spoke quietly, although her voice was tight, her breathing tense and shallow. "The reason the police wanted to speak to me in the first place was because my car had been seen near where she had been killed—up on Chapman's Hill."

"Yes, I remember that's what Jerry Francis told me," Mick said. "But you weren't—"

Sandy interrupted him. "No, I wasn't, but I knew right away what had happened. I knew it as soon as they told me that." She glanced over at the guard and lowered her voice even more. "Don't ever tell anyone, but I loaned Johnny my car that morning. It couldn't possibly have been anyone but him on Chapman's Hill that day."

Oh Jesus, thought Mick. What next?

Nineteen

THE GUARD CAME over to them. "Time's almost up," she said, but her voice was not unkind. Mick suspected she'd already let him stay longer than regulations allowed.

"Thanks. Can I stay a few minutes longer? We're almost finished," he said.

"A few minutes, then that's it," said the guard, and she returned to her chair by the door.

"I've got to be quick with what I'm going to say, Sandy."

"I know," she murmured.

"Does Johnny know you're here?"

"No. Mom told him and Paula I'd gone to Boston to visit my granddad."

"Then I've got to tell him."

"Oh God, please don't—you promised," she protested.

"No, no. Not what happened, not even that you confessed—just that the police arrested you. Don't you understand why?"

Sandy shook her head.

"If he were in this place, for something you did, would you ever be able to face yourself if you didn't tell the truth? If you let him rot his life away in prison for your sake? I don't think you'd let that happen. Would you?"

"No."

"Then Johnny deserves the same chance you do—to do what's right, I mean."

"Don't confuse me. I don't know what to do! I don't want anything to happen to him!"

"I simply want to tell him a terrible mistake has been made—that you've been arrested on some circumstantial evidence. And I believe as soon as I tell him that, I'm going to know whether he did it or not."

"How? You mean because he'll tell you the truth—to save my skin?"

"Yes," Mick said. "That's exactly what I think."

"But I don't want him to."

"Look, Sandy, suppose you're wrong," Mick pleaded. "Suppose the truth is that Johnny didn't do it? What do you think you're doing to him by spending the best years of your life in jail—years you could spend together? Think about it. Particularly if you're not protecting him at all, but someone else."

"Who could I be protecting? There is no one else."

Mick shrugged. "That remains to be seen. Christ! There *has* to be someone else. She must have had many enemies."

"On Dutchman's Island? I told you before, she'd never heard of the place until she met me."

"Well, I still haven't ruled out Evgeny, you know," Mick said, lamely.

Sandy also appeared willing to grasp at straws. "You really think I'm wrong, don't you?" she asked poignantly. "You really don't think Johnny did it?"

He took her hand and held it again. "I'm almost sure he didn't."

God, please let me be right, he thought. Just let me be right, and I'll never ask anything of you again.

"He's not there," she mumbled. "Johnny, I mean. He's not on the island."

"Where is he?"

"Down on the Jersey shore. He went down there to buy a new board and get a demo from the manufacturer. At least, I know he'd been planning to go down there now."

"Will you write down the manufacturer's name and where it's located?" Mick handed her a pen and paper, while the guard watched carefully. As soon as Sandy had finished, he said, "Now write down your lawyer's name and phone number for me." He watched her take a wrinkled business card from her pocket and obediently form neat and childlike script.

When she finished, he folded the piece of paper and tucked it in his wallet. "Okay, here's what I'm going to do. If Johnny tells me he is innocent, I'm going to call your lawyer right away, and he can start getting you the hell out of here."

"And if he's not?"

"That's up to Johnny."

She gazed soberly at Mick. "I'm so scared," she said.

"I know you are." He tried to smile, hoping to appear more confident than he felt. "You're a brave young woman, Cassandra Winslow. I think Johnny's damned lucky to have you."

"No, he's not," she said. "I'm not what he thinks I am." Tears filled her eyes.

"Listen," Mick said, "when things like this happen—Oh, hell! What I'm trying to say is it's common for the victim of rape to feel a goddamned load of unreasonable guilt, a lot of unreasonable shame. I think that's what happened to you, isn't it?"

She nodded sadly. "Maybe."

"Will you go for counseling, when you get out of here? Please, Sandy? For your sake, for Johnny's—for your mother and father's. Promise me you will?"

"You mean *if* I get out of here, not when."

"No," Mick rose from his chair. "You're wrong. I do mean when. Good-bye, Sandy. Thank you for trusting me," he added. "I won't let you down."

She reached across the table, grabbed his hand, and held it

tight. "Oh God, Mr. Merisi," she murmured. "I hope you're right."

"Please believe me when I say I'm sure I am," Mick said. "Everything will be okay. But now I've really got to go." The guard was watching them carefully.

She nodded. "I know. Good-bye."

She didn't look at him as he left and he didn't look back as the guard opened the door for him.

He heard Sandy burst into tears as the door was closing, but he thought these were the inevitable flood of relief coming after finally being freed of a terrible burden.

As he walked through the hall, which smelled of disinfectant and human misery, he thought about all the monstrous things he had heard that morning about the dead girl. She was a narcissist, but he had known that already. What he hadn't known until then was that she was completely mad.

He tried to imagine the pictures she'd taken of herself in the coffin. Was that a clue to what had really happened? he wondered. Did she believe so firmly in her own omnipotence that even death was something she could conquer and control? She had told Sandy she was "the dark side of the moon." Was death then simply a phase of the constant but ever-changing moon?

Could it also be possible she imagined that death by a handsome lover's hand might be the ultimate erotic thrill?

Suddenly Mick was frightened of what he might discover when he spoke with Johnny Selcott, but his inner voice told him not to think that way—not yet. He needed to hear whatever Sandy's boyfriend had to say with an open mind. And he wanted to be sure he heard only the truth—not the truth commingled with his own lurid fantasies.

Outside, the sky was hot and humid, leaden and heavy. He was glad he'd gotten the air-conditioning fixed in the van last month. He was going to need it on the long ride to New Jersey.

He pulled into a gas station, filled the tank, and used the pay phone to call Penelope.

"Oh, Mick—I thought you'd never call! What happened?"

"I'll tell you as soon as I see you. But I'm afraid that won't be until tomorrow. I can't explain why right now, but I wanted to tell you I think everything is going to be okay."

"Do you really, Mick? Or are you just saying that to make me feel better?"

"No, I really mean it. But that's all I can tell you. Except that your daughter is a good person, and I love you very much. I will love you forever."

He could hear her crying.

"Good-bye," he said. "I can't wait to hold you again."

"Hurry back—" she said. "I miss you so!"

He drove down the state highway for about ten miles until he turned right onto the ramp leading to the interstate. A heavy stench of diesel fumes surrounded him—the thundering noise of eighteen-wheelers. The air-conditioning was starting to fill the van with frigid air. Mick closed the window, and pushed the button on his tape deck. It was going to be a long ride.

He was shocked when Alfred Brendel began to play the opening movement of Mozart's great A Minor Sonata. Mick was sure he had disposed of that tape long ago on a highway in Arizona. He remembered tossing it out the window of the van, hearing it crunched by the wheels of some Navajo's dusty pickup truck . . .

But it must have been the wrong tape.

Suddenly he saw Claudia standing in the doorway of the kitchen in the studio. The same sonata was playing on the stereo, and he saw the same terror in her eyes he had seen in Sandy's that morning.

"Listen!" she had said, frowning. Her head was cocked warily—like some exquisite bird listening to another sing of danger somewhere in the dark, enchanted forest of her imagination. "Do you suppose Mozart knew he was going to die young when he wrote this?"

"Why do you say that? It's beautiful."

He had been outside, busy loading the van with his paintings.

He felt tired and hungry, yet also full of the excitement he always felt before any show—especially this one.

"Because I hear disappointment, heartbreak, so many things forever left undone. Don't you hear it, too, Mick?" She had closed her eyes and shivered. "Oh, God! The pale horseman—"

He had laughed, and taken her in his arms.

"What if anything happened to you? What if I ever lost you?" she had cried, clinging to him.

"Silly girl." He had smiled indulgently, and affectionately tucked a loose strand of hair behind her ear. "You can't get rid of me that easily!"

He had kissed her lips, but found them cold with fear.

That was the night before he had driven to New York alone to hang his show . . .

Mick was suddenly glad it had been another tape he destroyed—not this one. He could now imagine some blissful evening, after this nightmare was over, when Penelope would sit down at the Steinway in the cottage and play the sonata for him. For once again, he could hear its transcendent beauty conquering both death and disappointment—now that he had said goodbye to Claudia, now that her restless ghost had, at last, found peace.

As he recalled her grim premonition, he began to wonder if Claudia hadn't lured him back to Dutchman's Island, not only to say farewell, but also to fall in love with Penelope—and to aid the child she had loved and cared for, when that child needed someone's help and friendship. For Claudia had loved all three of them, and her soul was a sweet and generous one.

He pulled out and passed a slow car in the center lane. As he sped south past the roaring trucks, the eerie but magnificent "Presto" movement of the sonata began.

Twenty

IT WAS EARLY evening when Mick arrived at the Jersey shore. There was no wind blowing across the water. The setting sun hung in the gray, woolly smog blanketing the bay.

As he drove into the parking lot of the low building housing Hiroshige Sun/Fun, Mick had no difficulty spotting Johnny Selcott among the group of young men who stood idly sipping cans of soft drinks by the shore. They were uniformly garbed in black neoprene wet suits punctuated by occasional stripes or spots of high-visibility Day-Glo, but only one had the slightly feline stance of Evgeny Otkresta.

Sandy had been right. Their builds were indeed similar. Mick was surprised he hadn't noticed it earlier, for the years he had spent drawing from the nude model had trained him to rapidly observe, study, and evaluate the proportions, lines, and thrusts of a person's body. In fact, as a young art student, Mick had preferred working from the male nude, for the desire he occasionally felt while looking intently at an attractive woman's body sometimes destroyed the objectivity needed to make a strong drawing.

As Mick had noticed earlier with Evgeny Otkresta, Johnny Selcott, too, had the taut, yet graceful build of a skier or dancer—not tall, but with well-developed quadriceps and calf muscles. His shock of blond hair, bleached nearly white by the sun, gave him a superficial resemblance to the Russian. The somewhat sinister-looking black wet suit he wore also contributed to the effect. But up close the resemblance ended. Johnny had classic California lifeguard good looks, with none of the Tartar exoticism that had made Evgeny distinctive. Mick even found himself wondering what a sophisticated young woman with such bizarre and decadent tastes as Sabrina Ferris could have seen in Johnny Selcott. He certainly didn't have the beauty of the young man posing in her pastiche of the Arnolfini marriage portrait, the man who might be the same one who raped Sandy.

He introduced himself. "Hello, you're Johnny Selcott, aren't you? I don't know if you remember me—I'm Mick Merisi, a friend of the Winslows."

Johnny acknowledged Mick with a brief grunt and vigorous handshake.

"I was wondering if you're free this evening for a beer and something to eat?" Mick asked.

Johnny eyed him dubiously. "Sure," he said.

"I figure you must be wondering what the hell I'm doing down here. There's something important I have to discuss with you—something to do with Sandy."

A shadow of alarm crossed Johnny's face. "She's okay, isn't she? I thought she was in Boston with her granddad."

"Yes, she is. Okay, I mean. I'll explain when we find someplace to sit down and talk. I imagine you probably want to change before we eat, don't you?"

"Yeah. I'll just be a minute."

In faded jeans, a white T-shirt that bore the garish logo of SUN/FUN, and a cap with its visor worn backwards hiding his fair hair, Johnny bore no resemblance to Evgeny Otkresta. Mick was glad. He didn't want to think about the pale and putrid body he'd seen in the boathouse. He didn't want to think about Crosby's cries for help—those cries he hadn't heard.

They found a bar and grill not far down the road. It was one of many sleazy spots with blinking neon and garish chickens sitting in baskets that followed one another in relentless monotony along the highway. The roar of traffic was everywhere, drowning out any sound of the sea pounding the long, flat strip of sandy shore packed solid with bungalows and boardwalks.

"Sure makes you appreciate the island, doesn't it?" Johnny said.

"That it does," Mick agreed.

Inside the dark and smoky bar a couple of men with dingy, drooping mustaches and beer bellies were watching TV with glazed eyes, while another concentrated in serious solitude on the twinkling pinball machine.

Mick and Johnny found a quiet booth and sat down.

"As I said before, I guess you probably wonder what the hell I'm doing here," Mick said, after they had ordered draft beers and cheeseburgers, medium rare.

"You can say that again."

"I'd better come right out and tell you I've been talking with Sandy all morning. She told me I could find you here."

"You drove all the way down from Boston? How come?" Johnny peered at him suspiciously.

"I pushed it a little, I guess."

Mick had to be careful to remember that Sandy was supposed to be in Boston, a good three hours east of where he'd started from.

"So, what's up?" Johnny's question dangled in the air like the setting sun.

Damn these laconic Yankees, Mick thought.

He was relieved when the waitress brought two sweating glasses of cold, foamy beer. He took a long swig before speaking. It tasted good—like summertime and ball games long ago.

"A lot," he said. "Look, there's no point in my beating around the bush. Sandy's not with her grandfather, Johnny. She's not

154

even in Boston. Her mother tried very hard to keep you from knowing this—but she's in prison."

"What?" Johnny's voice rose. His face registered first shock, then horror, then disbelief.

"That's right. She was arrested for the murder of the girl I found on Wrecker's Point." Mick didn't take his eyes off Johnny as he spoke. He noted a flash of recognition, but the younger man said nothing.

"I'm trying to find out more about the girl's death," Mick continued. "Maybe I can bring some new evidence to the police that will get Sandy out of there. It's one hell of a mess. This is what they've got so far: a camera strap with Sandy's name tape sewed into it appears to have been the murder weapon; the cops found that out at the Point. Someone also saw her car on Chapman's Hill at about the time of death."

He decided against mentioning the note in the girl's pocket, fearing it would open up more inquiries into Sandy's story than he wanted to answer.

"It wasn't her," Johnny mumbled. "It was me. On the hill, I mean."

"What were you doing there?"

"Nothing much."

"Sandy means a lot to you, doesn't she?" Mick said.

Johnny stared blankly into his glass of beer and nodded. Only the persistent throbbing at his jawbone indicated anxiety or tension.

"Will you level with me about anything I have to ask you—and I mean anything? It's important. Please take my word for that."

"Sure. But I don't understand, Mr. Merisi. Why her?"

Mick shrugged. "The evidence seems pretty circumstantial to me. But apparently she knew the girl well."

Johnny started to say something, but no words came. He took a gulp of beer, then cleared his throat. Even so, when he spoke, his voice was forced and dry. "Yeah, she knew her from Arts and Crafts. That stinkin' place was full of freaks."

155

He finished off his beer. Mick summoned the waitress to bring refills.

"Did you know her, too?"

Johnny cracked his knuckles. "I never met her until the day Sandy came back to the island. That morning, she—Vanessa— stopped in at the boatyard, asked me to meet her on the beach in front of your place about eight. I didn't know why she chose that time and place, but since she seemed to be on the level when she said she was worried about Sandy, I thought I'd better go—figured I'd better find out what she had to say." He looked at Mick. "I've been sort worried about Sandy, too. Did she tell you she quit school? I know she hadn't told her mom or dad yet."

"No, but Mr. Winslow has hired a detective to supplement the police findings. She found that out pretty damned fast."

Johnny sighed. "Sandy told me she was flunking out. I took it for what it was worth."

"You didn't believe that was the real reason?"

"Maybe. Maybe not. I knew she was upset about something. But I figured she'd tell me about it whenever she was ready to. I wasn't going to push her."

The cheeseburgers arrived. Johnny poured a generous puddle of ketchup onto the rim of his plate and sunk a french fry into it. The random thought passed through Mick's brain that young Americans didn't deserve their apparent good health with such an infinite craving for junk food.

"Did you meet with the girl?"

"Yep."

"Can you tell me about it?"

"Rather not."

Mick sighed. "It's important, Johnny. Damned important."

Johnny curled another french fry expertly around in the ketchup, ate it, and took a bite of his cheeseburger before speaking. "She tricked me into coming down there. But she didn't want to talk about Sandy. No, sir," he said. "It was mighty stupid of me to bite on it."

Mick said nothing. He let him hesitate, waited patiently for him to continue his own account of the evening. But Johnny said nothing, instead concentrated on eating.

"Did you see me on the beach that night?" Mick asked, at last. "Because I was there."

"Nope. Didn't look."

"I saw you, but I mistook you for the Russian guy staying at the cottage." Mick turned his glass around and around on the table, idly making patterns of wet circles. Nothing connected, except those wet circles. "He's dead, too, by the way."

Johnny sat up straight and alert. "Anything to do with her?"

"Possibly." Mick shrugged. "The cops think it was a drug overdose. Sandy tells me the girl probably sold them to her."

"Maybe," Johnny said slowly and thoughtfully. "I wouldn't put it past her. She was a bad one, not to speak ill of the dead, you understand, but. Poor guy. I wondered what had become of him."

"What do you mean?" Mick asked.

"He wanted to have a boardsailing lesson with me," Johnny said. "He was set up for one the other day. Never showed up. I went up to the house and looked around, but I couldn't find him. I guess that's why. Poor guy," he repeated dolefully.

So it had been Sandy's boyfriend, not Evgeny Otkresta, Mick had seen stalking the green hill by the cottage with a panther's grace. His error in assuming it was the Russian had been compounded because Johnny hadn't been wearing his backwards baseball cap and he had been dressed all in black, just like the Russian painter.

"Why were you up on Chapman's Hill in Sandy's car that morning anyway?" Mick asked.

"Nothing special." Johnny blushed. "Nothing to do with *her*, that's for sure!" he added emphatically.

"Oh hell, Johnny, I'll stop beating around the bush," Mick said. "Just tell me the truth straight out—did you kill her?"

"Are you crazy?" Johnny's voice rose again, making the pinball player look up from his game. "Of course not!"

Mick smiled. "Thank God! I sure as hell didn't think you did. But I had to make sure."

He looked at his watch. Damn! It was too late now to call the lawyer. He pointed to Johnny's empty glass. "Another beer?"

"Shoot! I was going to try and drive back tonight, catch the first morning ferry—but—yeah, you bet I'll have another!"

Mick signaled the waitress.

The third beer seemed to make Johnny almost loquacious. "That girl was nuts, you know."

"That was the impression I got, too." The effects of the long drive combined with the beer were making Mick feel drowsy. "What did she do to make you think that?"

Johnny leaned across the table, spoke confidentially. "It's like this, Mr. Merisi. Even if a guy wants to make out with a girl— fool around—he still wants to be the one to do the asking. You know what I mean?"

"Sure."

"But she didn't waste any time letting me know that's what she wanted from me. She took that long dress she was wearing right off and didn't have a damned thing on under it. Not a damned thing!"

"You weren't attracted to her?"

"Hell, no! I've got a girl—the only one I'll ever want." He looked at Mick imploringly. "If I tell you something, will you promise not to tell Sandy? I mean, she might not understand."

"I won't tell her."

"Well, that girl suddenly grabbed me and reached into my pants pocket! I thought she was after something else—you know—but she took my splicing knife, opened it up, and said, 'How lovely! What a pretty little toy,' in that fancy, prissy voice of hers. Then, straight out of the blue, said she'd wished I'd *cut* her with it—stab her with the awl. Wow! I tell you, that bitch was *nuts!* A real freak!" He shook his head in disgust. "I was mad as hell. Sandy gave me that knife for my birthday—had it engraved with my initials, even. I know it cost a lot of money. That knife meant a lot to me."

"Did you get it away from her?"

"Nope. She started laughing like an idiot when I told her to give it back, and threw it down on the sand somewhere. I was scrambling around in the dark looking for it while she kept following me around and saying, 'Oh, Johnny, I've got such a lot to teach you!' Crazy bitch! Not a damned thing on . . . "

"Did you ever find your knife?"

He shook his head. "Sandy wanted to borrow it next day to splice a line and I couldn't think of a good excuse why I didn't have it. She knows I always carry it with me. I sure didn't want to tell her I'd lost it, but I don't think she believed me when I told her I'd left it home."

So that's what Sandy was doing the night Reynolds followed her. Looking for the knife.

"What happened next?" Mick asked.

Johnny's jawbone throbbed harder. He suddenly seemed older. "I don't usually talk like this, especially around girls, but I said to her, 'Go fuck yourself,' and left—went straight home to bed."

"And maybe that's exactly what she did," Mick muttered.

"I wouldn't know," Johnny said. "I walked away, and never looked back. That was the last I saw of her, I swear to God."

Mick looked somberly at Johnny. "The police may have your knife, you know. They searched that area pretty thoroughly."

"I thought of that. I've thought of it a lot, Mr. Merisi."

"Mick—"

"Mick." He took a bite of his cheeseburger, wiped his mouth, then continued. "I tried to tell Sandy what happened, but then she went crazy, too. She seemed to jump to the conclusion something had happened between me and that bitch. She didn't wait around to hear what I had to say—stormed right out the door."

"So she never knew what happened?"

"You mean she never knew *nothing* happened! Because nothing did! I was mad that she didn't trust me."

"Sure, you would be," Mick said. "Now tell me about borrowing her car."

Mick found the fact that Johnny was in the immediate vicinity of the murder that morning, at the time it was determined to have happened, more alarming than his meeting Sabrina Ferris on the beach. He wanted to hear a reason for it. Then it would all be over. Sandy would be free.

"You got any place to stay tonight?" Johnny asked.

"No, do you?"

"Yeah. I've got a room in a bed and breakfast down the road—didn't remember to check out yet. Just as well. There's twin beds, and coffee and doughnuts in the morning are included."

Mick found Johnny's gruff hospitality touching. "I was planning to sleep in my van, but a bed would feel great! I'm tired as hell. But you didn't tell me yet, how come you borrowed her car?"

Johnny cracked his knuckles again. "My dad had my Jeep in the shop overnight for a brake job. I had an early lesson scheduled at the pond, so Sandy picked me up at my house. It was a beginner lesson—some guy out here for the summer. There was a nice breeze, so I decided I might need a harness for him, and it was in the shop at the boatyard. I asked Sandy to start the lesson with the basics, while I took her car and went to get it." He tossed off the last of his beer, and nodded to the waitress.

"Two more here." Johnny pointed to the empty glasses.

Mick felt his eyes growing heavy. He wondered if he'd last through the finale of the story. He could have done with some coffee . . .

"Anyway, when I got to the boatyard, it was still closed, and I remembered my keys were at home. I decided to drive up to Sam's place to borrow his. But then, soon as I started up the hill, I looked out in the harbor and saw him out on the *Luna*, fussing around with his mooring. I figured he'd spent the night there like he sometimes does. I knew he'd be in soon, so I just took the car and went up old Chapman's Hill to kill a little time until Sam rowed in."

"Why, for Christ's sake?"

"No good reason." He smiled and looked embarrassed. "Sounds dumb, but I wanted to pick some roses for Sandy. She and her mom and—"

160

"Claudia, my wife? My late wife, I mean?" Mick realized he had never before referred to Claudia in that way.

"Uh-huh. They used to tend the old rose garden up there. I thought maybe Sandy'd like to have a bouquet—" He stopped abruptly.

"What were you going to say?"

"Did the cops really rule out that Girtin did it?"

"Yes. Why?"

"I was picking roses, and all of a sudden, I thought I heard a shot coming from that direction. I looked down at the shore, over at the dunes, but I didn't see anybody. I figured it must have been a car backfiring or something. But later, when I heard what happened, I figured, like everybody did, it was Tom Girtin. I mean, he's been threatening to do something like that for years."

"Did you tell anyone you heard it?"

"No. I kept quiet because I didn't want to get involved with the police. Not after—you know—that night."

In every way, Johnny Selcott revealed himself as a typical Dutchman's Islander—private, taciturn, mistrustful of outsiders, especially those in authority. Yet, Mick reflected, he seemed honest. And he seemed to trust him, which was good.

"I didn't think she'd been shot when I found her, Johnny," Mick said. "I eventually found out from Jerry Francis that whoever it was attempted to strangle her, using the camera strap. But there was a struggle in the water, so the actual cause of death turned out to be drowning." He recalled the girl's body lying on the beach—the seaweed tangled in her long hair. "When I first saw her, I thought she'd been crazy enough to swim in the cross-chop."

Johnny looked plaintively at Mick. "I sure wish her mom had told me what was going on. I feel awful—Sandy off in a place like that, and me not knowing anything, not one damn thing about it—not being able to help her in any way." His voice suddenly acquired the morose and self-pitying tone of someone who had drunk one too many beers. "I don't think she likes me—Mrs. Winslow, I mean. Did she say anything to you about me?"

161

"No. I don't think it's that she doesn't like you, Johnny. I just think she just wanted to stall—to buy Sandy some time and try to get her out of there before anyone, even you, found out about it. And you have helped her, my God, have you helped her! Go on," he said. "Tell me what happened after that."

"Not much. I went back to the harbor. Sam had come in and opened the shop by then. I got the harness, went back to the pond where Sandy and the guy were having the lesson."

"He's an alibi for her then, isn't he?"

"Oh, yeah. He was down there with both of us quite a while, asking a lot of questions about equipment and stuff. He's renting a place on the island. I forgot his name—Ted something—but it's in my book. I wonder why she didn't tell the police she was with him?" He frowned, then apparently decided the night was too late to ponder deeply into this.

At least she has an alibi, Mick decided. Thank God.

"Anyway, when I got back to the pond, I noticed I'd forgotten the stupid roses. I guess I put them down when I heard that sound, and forgot to pick them up again." Johnny grinned sheepishly. "I was too embarrassed to tell Sandy I'd gone and picked them, got my fingers pricked with thorns, and then been enough of a jerk to leave them there. So I never mentioned I'd gone up to the old place. I guess now I should have."

"Probably, but you had no reason to. No one could have guessed this was going to happen." Mick rubbed his burning eyes. "God! It's been one hell of a day! Go on."

"Sandy thinks I did it, doesn't she?" Johnny asked gravely. "But she's going along with the cops—letting them believe *she* did it, because she wants to protect me. Isn't that the way it is?"

"Maybe."

Mick looked into Johnny's eyes. They were deep brown, steady and candid. He had to level with him. There was no point in pretending otherwise, when Johnny had already guessed the truth.

"I'm afraid you've got it right, Johnny. That's why I had to know the truth."

"I see," Johnny said slowly and thoughtfully. "Anyway," he

162

continued, "we went back to the boatyard, worked on getting the rigging set on the other boards. As soon as we were done with that, Sandy went over to Pinkham's Market and got sandwiches for lunch. After the three of us had eaten—"

"Who do you mean by the three of us?"

"Me, her, and Sam. He was helping us. Anyway, after we'd eaten, she sailed around the harbor most of the afternoon while Sam and I worked on that old Herreshoff cat he's restoring for a guy off-island. And that's it—that's the whole story."

Mick frowned. "Sam was with you all afternoon?"

"Yeah, why? Until about four, four-thirty."

"Nothing. It's just that, after I found the body—while I was waiting on Wrecker's Point for the police to get there—I'm positive I saw the *Luna* sailing offshore."

"Couldn't have been. Must have been another boat. Sam was right there with me. And he doesn't let anyone else sail the *Luna*. Hell, Sam Palmer loves that boat more than his wife."

Except Claudia, thought Mick. He used to let Claudia sail it alone.

And it was the *Luna*. Christ, I'd know it anywhere.

C H A P T E R

Twenty-one

THE DAY DAWNED hot and humid as the previous one. Mick rolled over and saw Johnny sitting on the edge of his bed in his undershorts, rubbing his forehead.

"One too many?" Mick had lost count of how many beers they'd had. His own mouth felt like cotton.

"Maybe." Johnny looked at him and frowned. "There's something I didn't tell you. I couldn't stop thinking about it all night."

"What's that?"

"A buddy of mine works on the ferry. He told the cops Vanessa had come out to the island the Saturday before I met her. He also told them how she picked up the Russian guy on the boat that day."

"So?"

"Well, he told me something else. But promise you won't tell anyone—especially not the cops?"

Mick sat up on the edge of the sagging mattress and faced Johnny. "I think that depends on whatever you're going to tell me."

"Don't worry, it doesn't affect Sandy or me. Nothing like that.

It's just that my friend told me he'd seen her once before out on the island. She'd been out two weeks earlier. She was alone, had a rental car." Johnny hesitated. "But he never told the cops about it."

"Why not?"

"He was scared to. This is what I wanted you to promise you wouldn't tell anyone—he bought some pot from her. You won't mention that, will you?"

Mick lay back lazily on the pillow, gazing up at the brown water stain in one corner of the ceiling and the dimity wallpaper yellowing with age. He realized it no longer mattered to him that some young seaman had bought drugs from Sabrina Ferris. At least he knew now Sandy didn't kill her—and neither did Johnny. That was all that mattered. He was glad to be out of it, out of the whole mess of the young heiress's perverse life and violent death. Now he could return to Dutchman's Island and love Penelope—they could begin to make a life together. He had achieved all that he promised, and that was that.

Then she didn't just come out to the island because of Sandy, he thought. Some other business must have brought her there. But what?

It didn't matter what, he reminded himself.

"Oh, what the hell, Johnny." Mick yawned, sat up again, and stretched. "That doesn't matter to me now. Whoever did it is no concern of mine anymore, just the police's. I imagine they're going to have a hell of a lot of tracks to cover before they find out what happened. A hell of a lot—and maybe they never will discover who did it."

"He didn't. I know that," Johnny said, pulling on his jeans. "You know what, Mick?"

"No, what?"

"I don't think she was really a friend of Sandy's. I think she was just some creep who came out to the island wanting to make trouble for a bunch of hicks. She made some, and got some, too. Too much."

"Could be," Mick replied.

Now that he was fully awake, Mick was eager to be on the road. He hoped the antiquated and corroded stall shower down the hall worked. He felt grungy and stiff from the long hours sitting behind the wheel yesterday. The hot needles of a good shower would feel good. He rubbed his sandpaper cheek. A shave would help, too. Then he remembered his duffel containing clean clothes and his razor was sitting in the little room above the garage on Dutchman's Island.

It was almost seven. He could already smell coffee brewing downstairs in the parlor.

"I'm going to be on my way early," he said to Johnny, as he headed out the door toward the shower. "How about you?"

"Soon as I pack my board. Mick, do you think they'd let me visit Sandy?"

"I doubt if you'll have time to because, frankly, I think you're going to see her back on the island very soon. I'm going to call her lawyer as soon as he's available this morning. I hope he'll be able to work fast and get her home."

Johnny peered at Mick. "You know, I never asked you how come you did all this, anyway? I mean, it was a lot of trouble for you, wasn't it?"

"Like I told Sandy, Claudia loved her like a daughter. That's why."

Johnny ruminated on this a moment, then said, "Well, we're sure grateful—me and Sandy, I mean."

Mick said nothing, but grabbed one of the stiff and scratchy towels hanging on the door and went down the hall to the shower, humming to himself.

It was going to be a great day, in spite of the weather.

Twenty-two

"PENELOPE? WE'VE GOT a lousy connection. Can you hear me? It's Mick."

"Where are you?" She sounded a million miles away.

"A truck stop somewhere in New Jersey. I'll explain everything when I see you tonight—it's a long story. I just wanted to tell you that you'll be hearing some good news soon. I called Sandy's lawyer, and if she keeps her end of our bargain, she'll be withdrawing her confession."

"Is that true, Mick? Is it really true?"

"Yes—" The phone line crackled. They were cut off. He tried dialing the number again but the line was dead.

The sky had turned an ominous shade of pale umber. Mick wondered if he heard thunder, or if it was only the roaring of trucks. He got back in the van and began driving again. He was a long way from home. A hell of a long way.

Suddenly lightning ripped the sky, thunder drowned out the trucks, and rain began to come down in great, gray sheets. Even on their fastest speed the windshield wipers couldn't keep the glass clear. Before long, the six-lane divided highway became a river. Huge signs with flashing digital lights told drivers the speed limit on the turnpike had been reduced to thirty-five miles an hour.

"Jesus!" Mick muttered. He'd figured on four more hours of driving ahead of him under the best of conditions, and now this.

He suddenly saw scarlet brake lights go on in every car in every lane ahead of him, and hit his own brakes hard, skidding to a stop. The van hydroplaned and barely avoided swerving into a black chauffeured limousine in the left lane. Up ahead some gigantic unexplained shape sprawled across the road. In a few minutes Mick could see that a tractor-trailer had jackknifed, blocking all lanes.

State troopers eventually arrived and slowly guided vehicles along the shoulder to the nearest exit ramp, which led into some dreary brick factory town in New Jersey.

Rain continued to fall. When he saw a sign for the Holland Tunnel, Mick decided to drive into New York and wait out the storm while paying a long-overdue visit to his gallery. It would be good to see Helen again—to tell her he was back at work. He didn't have to tell her that, at present, to quote Matisse, he was only "painting without a paintbrush," mulling over images and storing those in his mind that might soon, with luck and hard work, find their way to canvas. For now Mick was eager to paint again. He knew he would, as soon as this was over.

Helen probably also had news for him on how the last *Wave* paintings were doing—news Mick felt like hearing for the first time in four years.

He parked the van in a lot in lower Manhattan, and scrounged around in back until he found his umbrella. When he opened it, Kitty Litter fell onto his face.

He ran through rainy streets, leaping over rivers and puddles, dodging pedestrians hidden under their umbrellas, until he came to the magnificent old Hooker's Green cast-iron building that housed the Helen Andokides Gallery.

It still looked the same: handsome wooden floors bleached pearly white, then softly waxed; pale, dove gray walls setting off all the colors in whatever paintings were currently on the walls. Graceful Ionic columns held up the antique tin ceiling and formed elegant, satisfying spatial divisions within the large room. On one cut-off column in a corner stood Helen's signature vase of white peonies, stained at the ragged edge of each petal with a faint touch of crimson. No one knew how she always managed to find them in every season. It was her secret.

An icily beautiful receptionist glanced up as he entered.

"I'd like to see Mrs. Andokides, please. Tell her it's Mick Merisi."

The ice goddess lost her composure for a brief moment. She picked up the phone and murmured, "Helen, Mick Merisi is here. No, really, I'm not kidding. He is." She glanced at Mick's two-day beard and damp, wrinkled clothes. "At least, that's who he says he is."

In seconds Helen stood before him. "You look great," he said, "as always."

She said nothing, but kissed him on both cheeks, making him again regret his inability to shave that morning. She took both his hands in hers and stood off from him—gazing at him, a faint and tender smile on her lips.

"Mick," she said, at last, "My God! So it's really you."

Helen Andokides was one of those women who had probably been too tall, too skinny, and somewhat buck-toothed when young. But at sixty she had turned these same attributes into distinctive glamour and poise worthy of a portrait by Bronzino. She always wore purple, with simple, bulky eighteen-carat gold jewelry, her shining white hair pulled severely back and tied with a narrow velvet ribbon.

In spite of her Greek name, Helen was one hundred percent WASP, from Evanston, Illinois. She had been a reluctant debutante, who had fallen in love with and married a Greek shipping heir. He had died too young of leukemia. Mick knew Helen had adored her husband. She had passed her youth as a wealthy but childless young widow, conquering her grief by studying painting in Athens, Paris, and Rome. But she had soon realized her greatest talent lay, not in her own work, but in having an extraordinary eye for the work of new artists. She had subsequently established herself as one of the hottest dealers in the New York art world. Helen managed her stable of artists with a mixture of maternal pride and ladylike but nevertheless sharp horse-trading.

"I guess you'd about given up on me, huh?" Mick said with an embarrassed grin.

"No, never." She looked at him solemnly. "I knew that one day you'd show up, and now you have. It's simply wonderful to see you, Mick. Do you have time for lunch?"

"Yeah, but—" He glanced at his watch.

"No buts, Micky, my love," she said brusquely. "It's so nasty out, let's eat in my office. Do you mind?" She didn't wait for an answer, but promptly picked up the phone and ordered Mick's favorite lunch from Dean and DeLuca.

He smiled. It was good to be back.

She opened her desk drawer, took out a lace-trimmed tablecloth, spread it across the desk, then festively arranged their simple lunch of a baguette, some garlicky pâté, a shapely bunch of Muscat grapes, and a bottle of Châteauneuf-du-Pape on it.

"Cheers!" Mick said, lifting his glass.

She clinked glasses with him, took a sip, savored the wine, then said, "I suppose you must know you're famous."

Mick said nothing, remembering the last time he was in the gallery. The crowds—the endless chatter—then finding that Claudia was dead.

"A dealer in Venice has just bought the four ebb tide canvases. Paolo is delightful. I think you'd like him. He wants to meet you."

Mick again imagined Penelope in Venice. The soft and luminous glow of the canals would set off her green eyes—those eyes the color of Venetian waterways on a clear day. He thought of how her fair skin and red-gold hair would reflect the ancient pink brick and creamy marble. Ah, to show her Giorgione, Bellini, and Titian in the Accademia—to watch her gasp with delight at the enchanted storytelling of Carpaccio. He decided he would take Penelope there as soon as summer was over.

"That's interesting. I'm actually thinking of going to Venice this fall," he said.

"Oh?"

For a moment Mick was about to tell her about Penelope. But he didn't—not yet. Instead, he changed the subject. "I'm planning a new series, Helen. I hope you'll like them. They're going to be quite different from the *Waves*. A lighter palette . . . " He shrugged, opened his palms, and smiled. "I don't know. You'll see."

"Can I plan on a show next September?" She looked at him, shrewd and sharp-eyed, and he knew she meant business.

He hadn't thought seriously until then of what his visit to the gallery meant—of the work that would lie ahead for him to be ready for a one-man show in just a little over a year. But, of course, if Helen had done as well with the *Waves* as she indicated, five years was a long time for her to wait for more. A hell of a long time.

He popped a grape into his mouth, ate it, and grinned. "Sure. Why not?"

In about an hour the rain let up somewhat. He left, feeling relaxed and happy. The good wine and garlicky pâté had gotten rid of the cottony taste in his mouth. Even the ice goddess said good-bye to him with something resembling friendliness.

Yes, it was good to be back among the living.

Something caught his eye in a small shop on the corner. There was a ring in the window. It was gold—contemporary, but with graceful swirls that recalled Art Nouveau form at its best. Within its largest curve nestled an uncut emerald, and on the crest of the little gold curl was a diamond, glittering through the wet windowpane. Like the canals of Venice, the emerald too was the color of Penelope's eyes.

Mick went inside and startled the serious young Japanese goldsmith working at his bench by offering to buy it immediately.

The goldsmith took the ring from the window and placed it on a small black velvet pillow. "Very nice engagement ring. I can make matching wedding ring, too."

"I'd like you to do that," Mick replied. "I'll call and let you know if the size is right."

He hadn't thought of it until that moment, but of course, that's what it was—an engagement ring. Penelope had said he should ask her again—to live with him in the cottage—when all the troubles with Sandy were over. And now they were. He would ask her to marry him as soon as he got back that night.

He watched the young man polish the ring with a soft chamois stained with jeweler's rouge, then he signed the credit card receipt, and put the small box in his pocket.

It began to rain again as he drove east on the New England Turnpike. Not as badly as in New Jersey, but hard enough to make him take it easy.

He pulled up at the ferry dock just as the thick hawsers that held it had been taken off the tarred black pilings. Mick shouted to the crewmen to wait. He waved his arms urgently, but the propellers only swirled the murky water sickly green and white, while he stood in the rain, watching the last boat of the day sail for Dutchman's Island without him.

A slight, nondescript-looking man was standing at the window, watching the dock, perhaps watching him. Another man stood nearby, facing the bow. A broad, powerful back was all Mick saw, but he immediately recognized that back as belonging to Reynolds. The man at the window could be no one other than his partner, Tony Caron.

Tony Caron, who, according to Jerry, still thought Mick was the one worth watching.

CHAPTER

Twenty-three

PENELOPE WAS GONE when Mick returned to the island next morning.

He found a brief note stuck on the door of his room over the garage. It said only that she had gone to bring Sandy home—that neither of them could ever thank him enough. Something about the tone of it seemed stiff and formal, until Mick recalled his few letters from her. That was the way Penelope always sounded when she wrote, he decided, as though she was uncomfortable with the printed word.

He smiled. She didn't need words.

He decided to buy some lobsters. He thought it might even be worth a trip back to the mainland to get a good bottle of Meursault. Two, in fact, since Sandy and Johnny might decide to join them in celebrating Sandy's homecoming—although Mick hoped they wouldn't.

But as he thought about spotting Caron and Reynolds on the ferry the previous evening, he decided it wasn't wise to leave the island, not right away. He didn't want to do anything to call attention to himself. He was sure the detectives were watching the comings and goings of all ferry and airplane travelers to and from the island.

He reasoned that maybe they were there because of the death of Evgeny Otkresta—that they were finally looking further into his role in the girl's life and death, as Mick had always thought they should. After all, the Russian artist could have had reasons for killing her. Perhaps she had refused to further supply his need for drugs, or perhaps he simply owed her money. Mick doubted that Trudy would have continued to be generous with pocket money for her protégé, once she realized he was spending it all on drugs. Yes, Evgeny still seemed to Mick the only other person on the island who had had any significant contact with the dead girl. Except for Trudy herself—and he didn't seriously consider that in her fragile health, she could have killed the graceful and lithe young woman who had struck Mick as a strong swimmer the night he first saw her.

He hoped the girl's death had been as simple as he was trying to persuade himself it was. Yet the stories Sandy and Johnny had told him hinted at something more sinister.

Why had she come out to Dutchman's Island two weeks before, as Johnny had told him she had? Who was she seeking out then? Not Sandy, not Johnny, for neither of them were there at that time. So someone else had drawn her there, and who could it have been but Evgeny?

His head ached. He wished Penelope would return. He wanted to be with her—he didn't want to think about the killing anymore. He wanted to live, to love.

Mick couldn't stop going over his conversation with Alain Dorfer. In retrospect, something about it now struck him as wrong. Perhaps the jovial gallery owner had known more than he admitted about the girl. Much more. Now that he thought about it, Mick decided it was quite strange that Dorfer hadn't appeared to know anything whatsoever about the recent death on Wrecker's Point. And it was suspicious, if he did know of it, that he didn't make any connection between the body on the beach and the unexplained disappearance of the artist whose work he was imminently planning to show. Perhaps Dorfer's seeming ingenuousness had been an act. Perhaps he knew Vanessa Bell or Cindy Sherman or Sabrina Ferris well—very well.

Mick decided to go down to the gallery in the harbor and talk to him.

As soon as Mick approached the gallery he was startled and alarmed to see that Dorfer wasn't alone. Caron and Reynolds were with him, looking intently and thoughtfully at pieces of artwork spread out on Dorfer's desk. Mick was sure he recognized Sabrina Ferris's pastiche of the *Naked Maja*.

He was able to turn and walk quickly away from the gallery before either of the policemen chanced to look up and see him, or before Dorfer himself could wave a hearty, smiling greeting.

Mick could imagine their conversation. Dorfer was no doubt telling them of his inquisitive visitor—the mysterious man named Mick—who had appeared to know much more than he himself did about the equally mysterious artist. No, the visitor had neglected to mention that he knew quite well where she could be found—in a police morgue somewhere.

Mick looked back on his conversation with Johnny, his meeting with Helen, with infinite nostalgia. The freedom he had felt only yesterday had vanished into a distant and unobtainable past. He now felt himself to be a prisoner on the island, a prisoner not only of his own paranoia, but of the two detectives' active return to the case.

He debated whether or not to tell them that he, at least, now knew who the girl really was. That might give them leads into the part of her life neither he, nor Sandy, nor anyone else he knew were aware of. The part in New York.

He suddenly regretted not telling Helen what was happening in his life at that moment, for it occurred to him she was likely to know Joanna Ferris—might even know her daughter. Might know who Dennis was.

But he decided against speaking to the detectives. There was no point in calling attention to himself. Best to stay out of it, if he could.

He considered stopping in at Vinnie's, but immediately guessed that was the first place they would make inquiries. Instead, he climbed into the van and drove the long way around the island, trying to think of what to do next. Sabrina Ferris's trail had led to Evgeny Otkresta, and now he was dead. It had led to Sandy and Johnny, and they were innocent.

He thought of what Johnny had told him about his friend on the ferry, but he couldn't convince himself that there was anything there except a kid who'd bought some pot from the girl. Dumb, but hardly grounds for murder.

He pulled into the driveway to check the messages on Penelope's answering machine. When Mick looked through the window of her office, he saw its red light blinking impatiently.

He pushed a button marked "PLAY."

A voice said, "Penelope—it's Mary. Can you call me as soon as possible, please? Thanks."

That was all.

He pushed another button that said "CLEAR." The machine whirred, then stopped. The red light stopped blinking, although it remained lit.

Mick went outside and sat in the porch swing. The daylilies in front of the house had begun to open. A swallowtail butterfly lighted on one. Somewhere, a woodpecker was drilling. A truck went down the road and he recognized Tom Girtin.

Had it been him? What about the shot Johnny thought he might have heard? Neither Jerry nor Reynolds had ever hinted at such a possibility. Was it really a gunshot Johnny heard, or simply a car backfiring?

Suddenly the telephone rang. Mick leaped up from the swing and ran inside. "Hello?" he said eagerly.

"Hello, is Mrs. Winslow there?" It was a woman's voice.

"No, I'm sorry, she's not. Who's calling?"

"I'm calling from Hogarth Marketing Associates. We're taking a survey of—"

"Sorry, I'm not interested," Mick said, and hung up.

He felt restless, and got back in the van and drove down to East

Beach. He felt like walking, feeling sea wind, spray, and sun on his face. The long, flat sand there presented no obstacles to fast walking—even jogging.

Now that summer had come, young mothers with small children were congregating on bright beach towels, surrounded by umbrellas, tents, coolers, water wings, plastic tubes, beach balls, and all the other gaudy paraphernalia required to take young children to the beach. Seeing them in bathing suits reminded Mick that he was still garbed in his city clothes—his prison-visiting clothes—a wrinkled seersucker jacket, tie, and khaki pants.

He walked past a volleyball game with college boys on one side, girls on the other. They stared at him as he passed, then laughed. He decided he was too conspicuous, that he should go home and change into jeans and a T-shirt.

There were still no messages on the machine.

After he sat down in the porch swing, a girl on a bicycle pulled into the yard. Mick thought she looked vaguely familiar.

"Hi," she said. "Mr. Merisi? I'm Paula, a friend of Sandy's. Remember me?"

"Yes, of course. Nice to see you, Paula."

"Golly, it's nice to have you back." She had a snub nose, big eyes, and a wide smile. Paula Potter had matured into the type Renoir loved to paint: decidedly overweight by today's fashionable standards, but with dark and luxurious wavy hair, tan skin, glowing pink cheeks, red lips, and white teeth.

"Are you looking for Sandy?" Mick hoped she wasn't. He didn't know how well he could cover for Sandy, not at this point.

"No, you. Mrs. Winslow asked me to let you know that she and Sandy are going to be staying at her dad's until tomorrow. I'm awfully sorry I didn't tell you sooner. She called early this morning, but I came around and you weren't here."

"They'll be back tomorrow?" He hoped the disappointment, the yearning didn't show in his voice.

"Sure thing. Have a nice day." She waved cheerfully, hopped on her bike, and continued down the road.

Obviously Paula still didn't know what was going on. Mick

wondered where Johnny was—if he had returned to the island yet. He remembered how Penelope had used the excuse that Sandy was with her grandfather in Boston to cover up where she was while in prison. He wondered if she was really there now, or if something had gone wrong, preventing them from returning to the island.

He considered calling Penelope's father, then realized he had no idea what the man's name was, or whereabouts in Boston he could be found. Penelope had never told him her maiden name . . .

But at least she would be back tomorrow.

Someone was mowing grass somewhere. It smelled good. Mick rocked the swing gently back and forth, leaned against the pillow in the corner, closed his eyes, and let the sweet, peaceful smells of summer mingle with memories of love.

Soon he was sound asleep.

C H A P T E R

Twenty-four

THREE DAYS PASSED, but Penelope didn't come back to the island. The red light on the answering machine never blinked.

Mick pulled into the Mobil Station. "Is Johnny around?" he asked Jack Selcott.

"Nope." He peered at Mick, squinting his eyes. "You're Mick Merisi, aren't you?"

"That's right."

"Heard you were back. Good to see you. I expect you want him to give you a boardsailing lesson."

"I thought I might give it a try." Mick was relieved that Jack had saved him from inventing some other reason for wanting to see his son.

"Check over at Palmer's in a day or so." Jack pulled out a thick wad of bills and made change. "Take care now."

Mick pulled into the parking lot by the ferry dock, and went into the pay phone there. He dialed the Holiday Inn near the prison, hoping on some remote chance that Penelope had left a forwarding address or phone number.

No one answered her room extension. Finally the desk clerk picked up the call.

"Hello, I'm trying to find Mrs. Penelope Winslow," Mick said.

"She left a couple of days ago."

"I see. Can you tell me if she left a number where she could be called? It's quite important that I reach her." It was a long shot, but it was always possible she had left her father's number for him.

"I'll check the computer, if you'll hold on a second. Here it is— Mr. Winslow paid her bill with American Express and checked her out four days ago. I'm afraid I don't see any number where she was going, or any forwarding address."

"Thank you." Mick hung up the phone.

He walked to the end of the ferry dock and watched the gulls wheeling and mewing around a trawler tied up in the harbor. He noticed that a number of new boats—sailboats and motorboats— were moored there now for the summer. He didn't know why the sight of the pleasure craft bobbing festively at their moorings made him feel even more lonely and despondent—and somehow betrayed.

Again he considered going to Vinnie's for a beer, then thought better of it. He didn't feel like talking to anyone, not now. It occurred to him he once again felt the way he had during his long wanderings, when he couldn't be with people at all, simply because they were not Claudia.

Only now they weren't Penelope.

"Mr. Winslow checked her out . . . " He kept hearing the clerk's voice saying that.

Could it be possible that their mutual grief and anxiety over Sandy had drawn Penelope and Chap back together? Mick couldn't help thinking of the story of someone he'd known casually in London, who was divorced and seemingly happily married for the second time. Then his child by his first wife had become seriously ill with something or other. The guy divorced the second wife, went back with the first—for the sake of the child.

But hell, Sandy wasn't a child! And besides, she was free, now.

Penelope's daughter strongly resembled her father, Chap Winslow, with his Jimmy Stewart good looks, his country club poise, quick smile, and unquestionable attractiveness. It was easy to see that the daughter Penelope loved so dearly was also Chap's child.

What if Penelope had only turned to Mick as a surrogate for Chap, as he, at first, had to her?

But she couldn't have faked what she seemed to feel for him. No one could.

He realized he didn't have any idea why Penelope and Chap had gotten divorced. She'd never told him, and he'd never asked. Jerry had said something about Chap's being a womanizer . . .

"Oh hell!" Mick muttered. It wasn't possible, he told himself again. She couldn't have given herself to him with such passion and abandonment if she was still in love with her ex-husband. No, it wasn't possible. She loved him, and no one else. And she had told him she would love him forever . . .

He walked over to the post office. Sarah Palmer was alone with her back to the counter, sorting mail.

"Hello," he called. "Anything for Merisi—General Delivery?"

She turned her head and lazily eyed a set of empty pigeonholes. "Doesn't look that way."

Mick knew how Sarah always took her time about sorting the mail. It was an island joke that the United States Mail was a notoriously inefficient way to reach anyone there.

"Thanks," he said, and left.

Before he knew what he was doing, he had returned to the pay phone by the dock. He took his wallet from his pocket and scrounged through the numerous business cards he'd accumulated over the past four years until he found the dog-eared one he was looking for.

I shouldn't be doing this, he thought.

He stuffed the card back into his pocket and walked out on the dock where the trawler was tied up. But he found that its stink of rotten fish made him vividly recall finding Evgeny Otkresta and Crosby—made him feel surrounded by death once more.

He walked quickly away from the boat, went to the phone booth, and dialed the number.

A woman with a pronounced New England accent answered on the second ring. "Newell, Norman, Winslow, and Andrews."

"Mr. Winslow, please."

"I'm sorry, Mr. Winslow isn't in."

"Can you tell me when you expect him?"

"He's out of town until next Friday."

"I see. Is there any way I can reach him? It's quite important." Fearing he would be transferred to another attorney in Chap's absence, Mick added, "It's regarding a personal matter. I'm a friend of his."

"I'm afraid he can't be reached. He's already in Bermuda."

Mick dreaded the next question he had to ask. He gulped to keep his mouth from being too dry to speak. "Is Mrs. Winslow with him, by any chance?"

The voice at the other end gave a brief, girlish laugh. "Well, I should hope so!"

"And Cassandra?"

"Mr. Winslow's daughter? No, she's not with them. Can I tell him who's calling? It's always possible he'll call in, although I don't expect him to."

"Just tell him Mick Merisi called. I'll try him again when he gets back. Thanks."

He said good-bye and hung up the phone.

So that was it. What he dreaded had happened.

Mick was surprised that he didn't feel anger, just a weighty and oppressive sadness, a feeling that the very air surrounding him was devoid of life-giving oxygen, a feeling that all color had suddenly drained from the landscape, a feeling that it would be good to fall into the welcoming sea and sink into its salty deep.

Of course, it had all been too good to be true. No man deserved to love and be loved by two women like Claudia and Penelope—not in one lifetime.

But he also asked himself if anyone deserved to so quickly lose both of them, as he had.

His feet felt as though they were made of lead as he trudged slowly over to the van. He got in, turned the ignition key, and wondered what would happen if he just drove onto the next ferry and left—just started driving west again, as he had four years ago. Or, better yet, what if he drove straight to JFK and boarded the next Air France flight?

He glanced over toward Vinnie's. He wanted a drink to help him decide.

As soon as he was halfway to the Clam Bar, the door of the restaurant opened. Two men descended the stairs: Reynolds and Caron.

Mick turned and walked quickly back to the van. He got back into it and pulled swiftly out of the parking area. He didn't know where he was heading at first. He reminded himself that he was, after all, innocent. Sure, they would want to talk to him again, and he would repeat his story. But if he fled, they'd find him— and his behavior might make him even more of a suspect than before. No, before he left, he had to resolve this mess, once and for all. Otherwise he'd spend his life in hiding, in fear they would knock on the door one day . . .

He considered going down to the police station and asking to speak to them right then and there, beginning to work aggressively toward assuaging whatever suspicions Caron might still hold.

But first, he'd check the answering machine one more time. Just in case she'd called, if only to tell him why she had done what she did, or to say she was sorry.

As if that would do any good.

He decided to check her mailbox, too. Perhaps she had written him a letter of explanation, but sent it in care of herself instead of General Delivery. He hadn't thought of that.

There was a catalogue from Talbot's inside the mailbox and one letter. His heart pounded when he saw it, and his hands shook so badly he dropped it to the ground. But as soon as he picked it up, he saw it wasn't for him. It was addressed to Ian Meer, in care of Mrs. Winslow. No telling how long it had been there.

He drove down to deliver it, for he felt as though he could walk no further. Every part of him was filled with a sickening yearning for Penelope, compounded with deep and painful humiliation.

He knocked on the door of the studio. Through the window he saw Stubbs jump down from the bed and rush to the door, barking his noisy greeting. Meer came out of the kitchen to see who was there.

Mick felt a sudden rush of adrenaline. It couldn't be . . .

But it was. The chase was on again.

The tall young man who opened the door was unmistakably the same one he had seen posing with Sabrina Ferris in the Arnolfini marriage portrait.

Twenty-five

MEER GLANCED AT the letter.

From the studio's wide picture window behind Meer, Mick could see the calm sea. The same endless and rhythmic waves washed upon the shore that the dead girl had ridden in the night Mick first saw her. The clear north light filling the room made Ian Meer appear as solidly defined and eternal as one of Piero della Francesca's grave and monumental figures.

Meer stared blankly at the letter. Only the raising and slight stiffening of his shoulders, a quick inward draw of his breath, revealed that he had any response to it.

As Mick looked at Ian Meer, he realized the element he had been seeking was now before him.

How had he managed to forget the lesson he'd always insisted his students learn: the essential lesson to be learned from studying negative space? For Mick knew that a painter always had to look as carefully at the space surrounding a form as at the form itself. It was often by seeing what *wasn't* there that whatever object at first had seemed to be the subject of a painting was finally fully defined.

It wasn't simply that Meer had apparently posed with Sabrina Ferris in the Arnolfini marriage portrait. No, he was also that previously unnoticed, but nevertheless significant element that made the entire composition Mick was struggling with come together—made it work.

Meer looked up from the letter. He stared at Mick. He looked dazed—as though he'd forgotten Mick had just given him the letter, as though he couldn't even understand why Mick was there. "Uh, thank you," he said and started to close the door.

Mick immediately put his foot on the landing, preventing the door from closing. "May I come in? I need to speak to you."

"Well, I—" Meer replied, confused.

"Please. It won't take long." Mick stepped inside and held out his hand to Meer. "By the way, my name's Mick Merisi. I'm the owner of this place you're renting."

"Oh, I see." Now Meer sounded relieved. "I suppose you want to discuss my vacating your studio before the lease is up. That's fine with me. Actually, I just finished writing a note to Mrs. Winslow telling her I won't be staying the summer after all."

Mick noted there was no longer any evidence of Meer's carvings in the room. It was, in fact, extremely neat, as though no one lived there. He noticed a bulging duffel on the floor by the bed.

"That's not what I want to talk about." Mick tried to make eye contact with Meer, but the young man looked away. "I want to talk about Sabrina Ferris."

"I don't understand—"

"I think you do. I saw you in a picture she . . . "

Mick was shocked at how rapidly Meer went pale, then staggered back and collapsed into a chair. He whispered, "What picture?"

So she was blackmailing you with her Hasselblad, too, Mick thought.

"What picture did you think it was?" he asked calmly.

Meer didn't answer.

"She's dead now, you know," Mick continued.

Meer remained silent.

"But you already knew that, didn't you?"

"Yes." The young man's voice could hardly be heard.

"Did you kill her?"

Meer didn't answer.

"I found her body on Wrecker's Point. I'd also seen her down on the beach in front of the studio two nights earlier. I didn't connect her being there with you, because I'd heard you weren't on the island at the time. But now I think she had come out here to see you. Why?"

Meer buried his head in his hands.

"Was she a lover? A former lover?"

"No."

"But you *did* know her?"

"Yes."

"Did you buy drugs from her?"

"Damn it! No!" Meer's voice rose angrily and for the first time he looked directly at Mick. His chest heaved and his voice was choked. "She was my sister. My half sister, I mean. Same mother, different fathers."

"Oh, Jesus," Mick murmured.

"You're right. She *had* come to see me. I never told her I was coming here. She found out by accident."

"How did she find out? Through Sandy Winslow? I know they were at school together."

"Indirectly. Mrs. Winslow telephoned her daughter and left a message that she wouldn't be able to meet her that Saturday for shopping since I was arriving early and she had to open the house for me. Sabrina was on the same dorm as her daughter. She answered the phone and took the message. Damn the bitch! Damn her!" The expression on his face was both terrified and terrifying. "What was the picture you saw? How did you happen to see it?"

"There's a new art gallery in town," Mick said. "She left some pieces of her work with the owner, hoping to have a one-man show."

"So she really meant what she said," Meer said sadly, quietly, as though speaking to himself alone.

"What do you mean? What did she say?"

"It doesn't matter. Go on."

"She left a picture of herself posing as the bride in a pastiche of the Arnolfini marriage portrait. You appear to be the groom."

"Oh, one of those." Meer sounded relieved. "I didn't pose for it. I have very little to do with her. She probably glued my face on someone else's body."

"But you thought I was talking about another picture, didn't you?"

Dorfer's information about how she had insisted on hanging the show herself—alone—was pulling the details of what had happened together in Mick's mind. The missing elements were appearing and a composition was forming. Sabrina Ferris had been planning to exhibit pictures as damaging to Meer as the ones she had taken of Sandy. Mick had figured that much out now. But that was all.

"Would you like some coffee?" Meer asked incongruously. "I was just making some when you arrived."

"Sure." Mick followed him into the kitchen. He was surprised that he felt no time pressure—no fear—felt that Meer would tell him everything when he was ready.

They soon returned to the large room, sat down at the dining table and drank their coffee, both silent at first.

"When I found her body, I seemed to be a suspect. I guess maybe I still am," Mick said. "The police are back on the island, investigating. That's why you might say I'm a very interested party."

He gazed at Meer, but saw only a blank. The young man's face registered nothing, but Mick saw a decided family resemblance to Sabrina Ferris, except that Ian Meer was, if possible, even more striking-looking than his half sister. He had a childlike and pure beauty—like one of those angelic beings invented by William Blake while dreaming of Michelangelo.

"She was here under an alias," Mick continued, "but I suppose you already knew that, too."

"I didn't, but I'm not surprised."

188

"There was another suspect—someone who has since been proven innocent."

Meer had no comment.

"Did you know the Russian artist living at the cottage for the summer?" Mick asked, deliberately jumping from subject to subject in hopes of catching Meer unawares, making him accidentally reveal something he hadn't meant to.

"No. I just came to the island to study birds."

So that ruled out any connection between Evgeny and Meer.

"He's dead, too—of a drug overdose. He and Sabrina had been seen together several times. I thought maybe he killed her. Do you think I could be right?"

Meer sipped his coffee and gazed abstractly toward the horizon. "Anything's possible," he said, finally.

"But you know I'm wrong in my supposition, don't you? I think you know who killed her—and why."

Meer sat back in his chair, seemingly preoccupied with opening the letter Mick had brought. As he read it, a faint, sardonic smile appeared on his face. Then he carefully replaced it in its envelope, looked at Mick, and said, "I'm sorry—what were you saying?"

"I said I thought you knew who killed her and why."

Meer said nothing.

"I'm going to have to call the police, you know," Mick said.

"Of course. I've been expecting you to say that before now." Meer slowly stirred a spoonful of sugar into his black coffee.

"Why did you do it, Ian?"

He gazed mournfully at the letter Mick had brought. "I didn't mean to. She made me. I'm sure you don't believe me, but it's true."

"No, I've found out quite a bit about her, and I do believe you," Mick said.

Stubbs began to whimper. Mick noted the same expression in the corgi's eyes as in his master's.

"What will happen to him?" Meer gently patted the dog until he lay down his head and was silent.

"I'll look out for him. We've gotten to know each other."

Meer smiled sadly. "I appreciate that."

"How did you happen to be sailing the *Luna* that day?" Mick asked.

"I wasn't."

"I think you were, Ian. I assumed it was Sam Palmer I saw offshore while I was waiting on Wrecker's Point for the police—after I found her body. Now I've found out he was somewhere else, with someone who can vouch for him. He couldn't possibly have been there."

Meer said nothing.

Sam never let anyone sail that boat, except Claudia, Mick thought. And he loved Claudia . . .

"You know Sam, don't you?" he asked.

A blank mask covered Meer's face. Although it was meant to reveal nothing, Mick interpreted it as hiding something.

"The man who runs the boatyard? I've seen him around."

"I don't think you're telling the truth," Mick said. "I think you know him quite well. He's a friend of yours, isn't he? A good friend."

Meer sighed—a sigh that seemed to rise from the depths of hell. "Everything's going to come out anyway. It probably already has." He shoved the letter toward Mick. "You might as well read this."

Mick took a two-page Xerox copy out of the envelope, unfolded it, and began to read. He had noticed that the letter was dated more than two weeks earlier, but the envelope was postmarked from New York only three days ago.

Dearest Mummy,

I think of you constantly and I miss you dreadfully. How is the trip? Is the weather glorious?

Even though I envy you the wonderful time you must be having, I'm glad I decided to stay in New York. The job is going absolutely fabulously! Ben is truly an inspiration. He's going to show me how to use the digital camera soon, which should be exciting. We are a marvelous team—I even suspect he's a tiny bit in love with me!

But enough about me—have you heard from Ian? I'm very, very concerned about him. I didn't want to trouble you by letting you know how worried I am, but I feel I must because, frankly, his behavior lately frightens me. You know how much I care about him. So you can imagine how upset I am to discover that he has again become involved with someone who can only harm him. Poor Ian is so sensitive—so vulnerable—but we know that, don't we? I just hope he isn't heading for another breakdown.

He isn't in Newport any longer, but instead is spending the summer in a funny, rather backward little place called Dutchman's Island. I didn't understand why he decided to go there until I went out to visit him a couple of weeks ago. I discovered he's met someone on the island and become dangerously infatuated with him. You know what I mean. This time it's a man who works in a boatyard—rather a surly but quite good-looking man.

Mummy, I'm worried sick. He won't listen to any advice I have—just gets angry and accuses me of all sorts of ridiculous, evil motives! Poor Ian! These romances with manipulative older men always seem to bring out his latent paranoia, which is coming to seem dangerous to me. If only he understood that I'm only offering my opinion because I love him.

Oh, how I wish you were here! I'm counting the days until you return. Ian is so deluded about everything. If I didn't know and love him the way I do, I'd say that, in his present state of mind, he might even be dangerous. I hate to tell you this, but he actually threatened to kill me if I did anything to try and bring him to his senses, such as tell you what's going on. So please—whatever you do, don't mention this letter to him. Of course, I know he didn't mean what he said—he couldn't have—but still . . .

Sometimes I wish we were like ordinary people. Ian

and I pay a terrible price for our wealth. The world seems full of greedy and opportunistic people, and he's such a naive and trusting person.

Anyway, enough said! It's time to go to work now. Miss you tons!

Please don't worry about what I told you. I'm sure this will pass and he will come to his senses.

Love and XXX
Brina

Mick folded the letter and replaced it in the envelope.

"I'm sure Mother's already on her way home," Ian looked sorrowfully at Mick. "May I tell you my side of the story? I know how much you loved Claudia—Sam told me a great deal about her, and you. You must know what love is—you even know what it is to fall in love at first sight. But you don't understand what it means to love someone and have to keep it hidden from the world."

"Go on," Mick said.

"I met Sam last fall. I was out here birding with an Audubon group, and went into the boat shop to buy a foul weather jacket because it started to drizzle. He took down my phone number from the credit card slip, and I knew he'd call. When he did, and we saw each other again, both our lives were changed—forever." He smiled nostalgically.

Mick wasn't surprised that Ian Meer was gay. In spite of having numerous gay friends, he still had the straight male's prejudice of assuming unusually beautiful men, such as Meer, must be homosexual. But Sam Palmer? Mick had always envied him his silent strength and virility—his machismo. He had even envied Claudia's lasting love for him, been jealous of it. But had that love only been the truest, most loyal of friendships, after all?

"We decided I should come out here to stay for the summer, so we could see more of each other—to make sure what we felt was real, and it was. Because of the boat, we could be together in secret. We had decided to leave soon, to take the *Luna* and head for the Caribbean—find a place where no one knew us, where we could begin a life together. Because, you see, Sam could never come out in the open here. He has been hiding for years behind the shadow of a wife he loathes, the memories of a girl he loved. The people on Dutchman's Island are very narrow-minded, you know."

"That they are," Mick agreed.

"That's why he decided to sell the boatyard to the man who runs the gas station, who wants to buy it for his son."

Mick recalled seeing Sam and Jack Selcott at Vinnie's. So *that's* what they were talking about, pushing papers about. Yet, to imagine Sam Palmer without his beloved boatyard—his island . . .

Ian studied the envelope that held Sabrina's letter, then put it in his pocket. "I had been on the mainland for a craft show two weeks ago. When it was over, Sam met me over there in the *Luna*. We were planning to return to the island that night, but an unexpected storm delayed us, so we sailed over at dawn. I swam from the boat to shore—down there," he gestured toward the beach, "and there she was, sitting on the beach, waiting for me. The sun was just rising," he added, for no apparent reason.

Ian paused and drank the last of his coffee. "Can I get you some more?" he asked.

Mick followed him into the kitchen. The cabinet door under the sink was slightly ajar, and he thought he could see Sabrina's tote bag hidden behind the garbage can.

When they returned to the dining table, Mick said, "She was blackmailing you, wasn't she?"

"How did you know?"

"Someone else, someone she was also blackmailing with erotic photographs, told me that was her hobby, so to speak. For some reason, she liked to reveal to the world those things that should be private. I understand she had taken pictures of one of her professors and his mistress, and was planning to exhibit them for the whole school to see."

"Then you know what she's like, what she's capable of," Meer said.

"I think I do."

Mick recalled his meeting with Sam Palmer at the water-lily pond—recalled seeing him pick up that small piece of orange paper or cardboard. Why hadn't he guessed then that it was part of a Kodak film box, and made a connection between him and the dead girl with the Hasselblad? Mick could see the piece of cardboard now—that unmistakable shade of Indian yellow.

"She had taken pictures of us."

"At the water-lily pond?"

"Yes. How did you know?"

"Just a guess," Mick said "It's a very private place. I used to go there with Claudia, long ago." He paused, remembering that secret Arcadia. "You thought Sabrina was planning to exhibit the pictures—here, where everyone knows Sam?"

"I *knew* she was going to. She told me so. She'd already arranged for a one-man show of them at some gallery on the island." He paused. "I couldn't let her do that."

"Because of Sam?"

"Yes. You see, he's always thought that loving men was like a disease—something to be ashamed of—something he could be cured of. That's why it hurt him so when Claudia broke off with him."

"She knew?"

"Yes. She was the only person he ever told. But he loved her, and thought she was the woman who could cure him, so to speak. He has told me a great deal about her. He said she was born with more wisdom than most people acquire in a lifetime. I guess so, because even though she was just a kid, she knew otherwise. She knew he couldn't change his essential being—he shouldn't even try to. He didn't believe her, but she was right. Such things always end badly." He closed his eyes and sighed. "I only wish Sabrina had been as wise."

"What do you mean?" Mick asked.

"She has wanted me to make love to her for a long time, since she was twelve years old. That's why I avoided her—one of the reasons, I should say."

194

So this is like the dreadful end of the myth of Orpheus, Mick thought. Where the Furies killed and decapitated the poet because, having lost Eurydice, he could never love a woman again. That gruesome myth that only story and song can tell, not painting—it is too horrifying for the actuality, the physical nature of the art form. Except it was Sam Palmer, not Ian Meer, who lost his Eurydice forever in the Underworld.

"I should be shocked," Mick said, after a while, "but nothing I hear about her shocks me at this point. I can well understand how such a narcissist as she was would be attracted to a man who so resembled her. You look more alike than most siblings of the same parents. I suppose you know that."

"So they say. Even though I was only seventeen, I already knew I wasn't attracted to women. There was someone I cared about—someone who cared about me—and that's how I first discovered how dangerous Sabrina's little spy games were. She found out, and told Mother." He smiled sardonically. "Our loving mother immediately arranged that I be hospitalized for a nervous breakdown to help cure me of my 'sickness.' "

"How the hell did she manage that?"

"Oh, she had ways. When you're a generous contributor to numerous mental health organizations, you can pull quite a few strings. And Mother did just that. Actually, it wasn't all bad. That's where I learned to carve, as a matter of fact. And I had a wonderful doctor. I'm afraid poor Mother's cure had the opposite result from what she'd planned, because, with his help, I came to terms with the way I was." He sighed. "God! How I wish Sam had . . .

"Anyway, Sabrina and I started walking up the beach together," Ian continued. Like Sandy, he, too seemed to want to rid himself of the terrible tale, no matter how painful relating it was. "I didn't want her to come into the house where I lived. I had been so happy there."

As I was, Mick thought.

"All of a sudden, as we were walking, she pulled these pictures out of her bag—pictures of me and Sam. Pictures of something beautiful that she had made appear ugly, shameful. I tried to get them away, but she put them back in the bag, held it tight under her arm. I walked ahead of her, trying to figure out how I could get those photographs from her without hurting her, and all of a sudden I heard a shot. I turned around and saw that Sabrina had this damned pistol in her hand, and had fired it into the air. 'I could kill you, you know, Ian,' she said, smirking, so I grabbed the gun from her, but as soon as I did, she took my picture holding it. Then I tried to get the camera away from her, but she took it off the strap and threw it down the beach, laughing."

"The zipper of her shorts was undone when I found her," Mick said. "Why?"

"I think she was starting to undress—to tempt me—I don't know. I didn't notice that, frankly. As soon as she threw the camera away, all I could see was that the strap was still around her neck, and I was so angry I grabbed it, and we started fighting like we did when we were kids. Look—" He showed Mick some long scratch marks on his arms, and high up on his left bicep, a green and yellow bruise and the faint signs of tooth marks.

"She bit you?"

"Yes." He pulled down his sleeve to hide to bruise. "Then she started pulling both of us backwards into the surf, laughing at me, mocking me, calling me names, and before I knew it, I twisted the camera strap and pulled it tight around her neck, and—oh God!" he moaned. "Why didn't she just mind her own damned business? Stay away from me?"

"But she died of drowning," Mick said.

"I guess so. Suddenly we were in deep water and I still had hold of the strap. She seemed to be unconscious. A wave grabbed her, pulled her from me, and I couldn't get hold of her again. I swam in to shore. I'm quite a good swimmer," he added modestly.

"You must be." Even Claudia would never have dared swim there.

"When I got to the beach, I could see her drifting off, not doing anything to try to make it to shore. Then I knew she was dead."

196

"It could have been an accident. After all, there have been numerous drownings there."

"It wasn't an accident. It was exactly what she wanted. Exactly the way she planned it," Meer said solemnly. "Her letter proves it."

Wouldn't it be possible to prove in court it had been an accident? Mick wondered. Anyway, her death was certainly manslaughter, not murder . . .

He didn't understand why this young man aroused such sympathy in him. But he did. Ian Meer's idea that Sabrina had willed and even plotted her own death seemed alarmingly likely to him. Since she had apparently arranged with someone in New York to mail her letter to their mother some time after her rendezvous with her half brother on the island, it appeared she was making certain he wouldn't get away with killing her—by telling their mother he had threatened to. Worse yet, from Ian Meer's point of view, Sam, too, would be implicated after their mother received the letter, if she hadn't already. And it was clear to Mick that the young man wanted to protect the person he loved as much as Sandy had.

"Anyway," Meer continued, "I didn't know what else to do except pick up her beach bag, camera, and gun, and head for home. I don't think it had even sunk in yet that I'd killed her. But when I got back to the house I realized I hadn't brought the strap with me, so I started running back to Wrecker's Point to get it. By then, I knew I had to be careful. I had so much to live for, you see . . . "

"You ran barefoot along the water's edge so no one could follow you?" Mick asked.

"Yes. That way, no one would know I'd been there." He looked down at Stubbs. "Then I thought I heard this little guy off in the distance, and thought it was all over—that he and Cathy Girtin would see me, so I didn't go back to the point. I just dived into the surf, and swam over to where *Luna* was moored. And I knew then, I would be running from her forever."

"Do you believe that the terns took the strap up into the dunes? Or do you think Cathy saw the body?"

"No. I think the birds might have done that. As soon as I reached the boat, I thought I'd better go out and see if I could find Sabrina's body offshore, try to sink it, or get rid of it somehow. But I'd never sailed *Luna* alone, and it took me longer than it should have to set sail. I had to tack over there, and by the time I was off the Point I didn't see her in the water anywhere." His eyes met Mick's. "I thought—I hoped—at first that her body had somehow sunk, but then I saw you standing on the beach. I looked through my binoculars and saw that you had found her."

C H A P T E R

Twenty-six

IAN LOOKED AT Mick with despair. "Since then, I see her everywhere, I hear her taunting me. Out on the boat, she whispers from the water, laughing at me, laughing at us. There is no place on earth I can hide from her."

Mick didn't say anything. He knew what it was to be haunted.

"Sam hid me out on the boat," Ian said.

"So he knows?" Mick said.

"Yes. He guessed something was wrong when he realized I'd taken the *Luna* out that morning; and when he heard of the girl's death, he suspected what had happened. I made the mistake of telling him everything. Then he heard a rumor that an arrest had been made. He didn't know who it was, but it seemed safe for me to show up, safe for us to leave quickly for somewhere else." He smiled sadly at Mick. "We almost made it, you know."

"I know. I think you probably would have, except for me," Mick said. "I'm sorry. But I've got to call the police now, Ian. I wish I didn't, but you know I do, don't you?"

Meer nodded. "Yes, of course. I expected you to. I'm not sorry.

I never would have escaped her." He looked at Mick imploringly. "But don't tell them he knew about it, please?"

"I won't tell them anything except that you admitted killing her."

Now that Meer knew the police would inevitably come, he seemed sweet, tranquil, and childlike—trusting. His docility pained Mick, made him wish that he could scrape out all that he'd heard, as he did a section of a painting that didn't work. But that wasn't possible.

"Listen," Mick said. "Do you know of a good lawyer?"

"Oh, yes. Mother's friends are always the very best at what they do. Philip Brunello is an old family friend. I assume you've heard of him?"

Mick recognized the name—a flamboyant celebrity criminal lawyer who took impossible cases and usually won, the Clarence Darrow of today.

"I certainly have. Please promise me you'll call him before you tell them anything, will you?"

"Yes, I will," Meer said. "May I make one other phone call first? In private?"

"Of course."

Meer went into the kitchen and closed the door quietly behind him.

A few moments passed, then something occurred to Mick . . .

"Oh, Jesus!" he cried, jumping up from the chair. He ran toward the kitchen and reached the door just as the shot was fired.

Ian Meer lay on the kitchen floor in a rapidly spreading pool of blood surrounding his head and shoulders. Sabrina's tote bag lay beside him. For some odd reason, Mick noticed it was a Fendi bag—quite expensive.

The blood was already darkening the place where salt had stained the beach bag white. Her Hasselblad lay tumbled half out of it, its shining metal corroded green and white. Ian's face was strangely peaceful and even more angelic in death.

When Mick went over to the telephone to call the police, he noticed a burnt match lying on the kitchen counter. He looked into the garbage can. The white plastic bag lining it was empty except for a few shreds of charred ashes. Mick knew it was the remains of Sabrina's letter to their mother.

As he gave the grim news of Ian Meer's suicide to Sergeant Diaz, Stubbs entered the kitchen and began to sniff around Meer's body.

"Out!" Mick shouted, and the little dog ran off in humiliation.

Mick left the kitchen and closed the door. He sat down in one of the Stickley chairs and waited for them to arrive. Stubbs came and lay beside him, whimpering. Mick patted him, a feeble attempt at comfort.

Soon the police car with flashing lights pulled up on the lawn, followed by Caron and Reynolds in their plain and dusty brown sedan.

"He's in there," Mick said, pointing toward the kitchen.

Caron accompanied Sergeant Diaz and George into the kitchen, while Reynolds came over and sat down across from Mick.

"Can you tell me what happened, Mr. Merisi?" he said.

"Goddamn it!" Mick exclaimed. "I never should have let him go in the kitchen alone. He had just finished telling me he killed the girl I found on Wrecker's Point—told me how it happened. He knew I was going to call you!"

"He killed Vanessa Bell? Is that what you're telling me, Mr. Merisi?" Reynolds said eagerly, his calm mask dropping away for a moment at this news.

"Yes."

"Go on, please, Mr. Merisi."

"Her real name was Sabrina Ferris and she was his half sister. From what he told me, it was apparently a family quarrel going way back. It appeared to be self-defense. Apparently she aimed her gun at him when they were walking out on Wrecker's Point. She was a drug dealer, you know—"

"Yes, we found that out," Reynolds said.

"I guess that's why she carried a gun. Meer managed to take it away from her, and a struggle followed. Goddamn it!" Mick hit the arm of the chair with his fist. "I should have guessed the damned gun was still here."

Reynolds put away his notebook and his voice was kind. "You can give us the details later."

Mick wanted Penelope. He wanted to lie down beside her—to let her comfort him for the pain he felt. That would never happen now, he knew that. He would never hold her in his arms again. Yet he could think of nothing else. The tragic irony that he would never have found the letter—would never have been there with Meer—would never have recognized his face from the Arnolfini marriage portrait had he not been looking, no, hoping for word from her, struck him for the first time.

He stared out the window at the calm and limpid sea. He thought of both the women he loved: Claudia, who lay dead in its depths, and Penelope, who was now probably strolling barefoot on another of its shores, in the warm, frothy, turquoise water and pink coral sand of Bermuda, hand in hand with her husband.

As he went over his answers to the few questions Reynolds had asked, Mick realized that nothing he had been required to say to the detective had even hinted at Sam Palmer's unwitting role in the grotesque life and death of Sabrina Ferris and her half brother. He was glad. Claudia had protected Sam's secret from the world's eyes, and now he would, too. That was his legacy from her—and his assurance to her soul that she could always trust him. But he would tell Sam of his talk with Meer. He would tell him how much the young man loved him. He thought Sam needed a friend, a confidant. He always had, ever since Claudia had been gone.

Then he remembered that the charred paper in the garbage can was only a copy of Sabrina's letter to their mother. Perhaps Joanna Ferris had already read it . . .

Sergeant Diaz came out of the kitchen and said to Reynolds, "Tony wants to speak with you for a minute."

"Sure." Reynolds got up and followed her out of the room.

As Mick continued to gaze out the window at the water, he saw a breeze come up. He watched it fill the sails of a boat lumbering in the dark sea's calm swells, its gaff flopping awkwardly in the calm.

As the mainsail suddenly took the wind and the boat began to sail swiftly away from Dutchman's Island, Mick realized it was the *Luna*.

CHAPTER

Twenty-seven

MICK HAD JUST finished packing the last portfolio of drawings in the van. Helen would be pleased. It would make a decent show in September. Nothing like the *Wave* series, but nevertheless a signal to the art world that he was still alive and kicking.

Something tapped him on his sandalled foot. Stubbs was holding a stick in his mouth, patiently waiting for Mick to throw it. He didn't have the heart to say no again. It was good to see him wanting to play instead of lying miserably moping in a corner alone. The poor dog was obviously grieving for his former master, reminding Mick of yet another aspect of love. This game of throwing sticks was his way of bonding with a new friend.

Mick couldn't seem to think of much lately besides the many variations upon the tragic theme of love. He had been involved with so many manifestations of it recently—too many. Sandy and Johnny, himself and Claudia, Ian and Sam, Penelope and himself, Sabrina Ferris and Ian—not to mention Penelope and Chap.

Oh hell, he thought. Better not to think about that.

He picked up the stick, tossed it far across the lawn, and Stubbs took off in eager pursuit. He returned with it and dropped it again at Mick's feet. But this time, he didn't wait for Mick to throw it. Instead, the dog suddenly took off down the road, barking at someone or something.

Probably another cat, Mick thought, and climbed the stairs to the deck of the studio.

It was remarkable how quickly Sergeant Diaz and the crew of helpers she gathered together had taken care of cleaning up after Ian Meer's suicide. Not that Mick wanted to live there. No, he could never live there again. But at least now he could remove his artwork without seeing bloodstains on the kitchen floor, although he would never forget the terrible afternoon when the young man had confessed to him, then shot himself.

All that was left now were a couple of sketchbooks. Mick thumbed through one of them—it was full of casual sketches of Claudia. Claudia sleeping, Claudia dancing, Claudia eating, Claudia cooking, Claudia playing with Crosby . . .

God! What a life they had together. Short, but glorious!

"Mick?"

He turned around quickly. Penelope was standing at the screen door. She was dressed in a short cover-up of white terrycloth, and was looking even more beautiful than he remembered.

She came into the studio and touched him on the arm, "Mick?" she said. "I'm back."

"So it seems," he commented. "Excuse me." He walked past her out onto the deck. Just the feel of her fingers on his arm had been enough to make him inappropriately desire her.

She followed him. "Mick, please don't be angry at me. I'm sorry I couldn't reach you. I wrote you two letters, one in care of General Delivery and one to my box, but you never got them, did you?"

"No."

"I drove back from Boston with Johnny yesterday, but you weren't here. I guess you probably didn't get my letters because of Sarah. You've heard about Sam, haven't you?"

"No. I've been in New York. Why? What happened?"

"It's so horrible . . . " Tears filled her eyes. "Johnny is so upset. He worshipped Sam."

"What the hell are you talking about?"

"He was out in his boat, and some sport fishermen out trolling noticed it was drawing water and sinking fast. They got over to it just as it capsized." She turned away, and when she spoke again, her voice was tight and choked. "They tried to rescue him, but he had tied . . . Oh God!"

Oh Jesus, Mick thought. I don't want to hear what she's going to say!

"He had tied a large net bag of stones around his waist. He went down quickly, and apparently didn't try to swim at all. When the boat went over, they could see that several holes had been carefully cut in its bottom. They radioed the Coast Guard, but when they got there, they found nothing. Nothing at all. Some divers went down, but they couldn't find him. It happened in very deep water."

"Oh Jesus! Oh Jesus!" was all Mick could say.

"That was three days ago. No one knows why he did it. Mick," she touched his arm again. "You're going to hear this eventually anyway, so I have to tell you what Sarah is saying."

"What?"

"She's telling everyone in town he did it because he never got over pining for Claudia. She's making it sound as though something had been going on between them when she died. But that's not true, Mick. I know it isn't. Claudia would never have done that to you."

"They were good friends, that's all," Mick said. "It doesn't matter what Sarah says. If it makes her feel better to believe that, that's okay with me." He shrugged. "Claudia did love Sam, but not in the same way she loved me. Oh Jesus—poor Sam."

"He was a very lonely man," Penelope said sadly. "There's going to be a memorial service tomorrow. Sandy's coming down for it, and Johnny's planning to read a poem for him."

"I'd like to read something, too," Mick said. "Something of Claudia's."

He thought of Sam's smiling photograph in the Colette novel in the closet in the cottage. He wondered if his French was good enough to translate a passage from it. If not, he would surely find something else appropriate among Claudia's books.

"It's strange—Johnny just told me yesterday his dad was in the process of buying the boatyard. I couldn't believe it. I wonder why he was selling it? Sam loved working on those old boats. That was his whole life." She looked off over the water. "I guess now we'll never know, will we?"

It had happened the day Ian Meer shot himself, the day Mick saw the *Luna* sail away. To safety, he had hoped.

"Mick?" Penelope said. "Please don't be angry at me. I'm sorry I couldn't manage to tell you where I've been, and I'm sorry everything took longer than I'd hoped." She took a small tape out of her pocket. "This was broken—that's why I couldn't leave a message for you on the answering machine. Then, when Paula came up to see Sandy and I couldn't use her to contact you, I left a message with Vinnie, but I guess you never showed up there."

"No. As I said, I've been down in New York for the last few days. I've been staying at my dealer's place and trying to get ready to go to France next week."

"France? Why, Mick?" She began to cry. "I thought—I mean— remember what you said about us, about living in the cottage?"

"Of course. But you were right to suggest that I ask you again when all this was over."

"No." She looked at him angrily. "I don't think I was right. I only said that because I was afraid you'd change your mind, and now you have." She headed for the stairs.

"You're back early, aren't you?" he couldn't resist calling after her. "How was Bermuda, by the way?"

"Bermuda?" She turned and looked at him, wiped her eyes with the back of her hand, and frowned. "Mick, I really don't know what you're talking about."

"Penelope," he said wearily. "Come on. I called Chap's office. I know all about it."

"All about what?"

"Your going to Bermuda with him."

Don't let her lie to me on top of it, Mick thought. Don't let her treat me like a fool.

"Are you completely out of your mind? Me going to Bermuda with Chap? What on earth gave you that crazy idea?"

"I called his office to see if he knew where I could reach you and was told he was in Bermuda until Friday of this week. I asked if you were with him, and the receptionist said yes. That's it. Then I understood why I hadn't heard from you."

"She told you I was with him?"

"I asked if Mrs. Winslow went with him, and she said yes."

Penelope's puzzled frown suddenly turned into a broad and radiant smile. "Oh, my lord! Now I get it! Sandy was right! She told me she thought there was a lot more than a professional relationship between Chap and the lovely Marina. Wow! They must have married! Apparently she'd recently gotten divorced. I guess, considering what Sandy's been through, they must have felt it was not the time to tell her what they had been planning, just like I did about us." She came back up on the deck and stood before him. "Oh, Mick, how terrible that must have been for you—thinking I was with Chap all this time!"

"You mean you really *were* with your father?"

"Of course I was. Oh, it's so complicated, Mick. I almost don't know where to begin. Dad's been having these angina attacks for quite a while, and on the very day Sandy got out of prison, I found there was a message on my tape from my sister-in-law, Mary."

"I heard it."

"Well, she was trying to reach me to tell me that it had gotten worse and he'd finally agreed to go ahead with bypass surgery. In fact, the doctors told him it needed to be done right away. So as soon as I'd spoken with Mary, Sandy and I headed straight up there and we've been with him in the hospital in Boston. He's fine now—absolutely fine—and will be home soon. Sandy has decided to stay with him while he recuperates. He could use some help with shopping and housework. Also, she's decided to go for some counseling with someone—a psychologist—in Cambridge."

"Good," Mick mumbled. "I'm glad."

"She never did tell me anything about her relationship with the girl," Penelope continued, "and I didn't ask what happened to make her confess to killing her. She just said she'd learned a lot about herself through talking with you, and thought she needed some professional help."

Penelope looked at Mick with that expression of tender expectation she had worn the morning he said good-bye to Claudia, and said softly, "She thinks the world of you, Mick. So does Johnny, and of course, so do I." Her wide grin returned. "In fact, you might not care to hear this, but so does Chap."

Mick wanted to take her in his arms, but he couldn't. He felt too humiliated that he'd revealed his unfounded jealousy, his weakness of jumping to conclusions too quickly. That was something he'd have to work on. He was reminded of how he'd always suspected Claudia of still loving Sam. It had been the only friction in his love for her. And if it hadn't been for Helen Andokides's kindness and hospitality to him these past few days, he would already be far away in France—gone for good from Penelope. For it was Helen who had listened to his story, Helen who had advised him to talk with Penelope before he left. To at least hear her explanation of the situation.

Damn it! he thought. How can I be such an idiot?

"Mick?" Penelope's voice was soft, tempting. "I'll always be grateful for what you did for Sandy, but I'm rather sorry you got into the habit of thinking like a detective all the time." She smiled tenderly at him. "How could you have ever thought I could be with Chap? Didn't you have any idea how much I love you?" She paused. "I said I'd love you forever, remember? That nothing could change that?"

"Of course I remember. And I love you so." He turned away. He couldn't look at her. He felt he wore his shame too openly.

"I told my dad about you," she said shyly. "I wanted to be sure he knew about us—knew how happy I was—in case anything happened to him. Now he can't wait to meet you. I think you'll like him."

Mick was silent. Penelope gazed at him quizzically.

"Mick?"

"What?"

"You never asked me why Chap and I got divorced. Weren't you at all curious?"

"None of my business, I guess," he mumbled.

"Oh, but it *was* your business. Very much your business. You see, Chap and I might never have stayed married if we hadn't had Sandy, because I never loved him. I discovered that right away. It wasn't his fault. I married him when I was much too young— only eighteen, and a very innocent eighteen at that. He was considered a catch by all my friends in college, and when he preferred me, asked me to marry him before he went off to law school, I was flattered. But I never felt for him what I feel for you. Never." She paused. "Do you remember about a year and a half ago when you wrote and said you'd be coming back soon?"

"I guess so."

"You never came, but the day I got your letter was the day I asked him for a divorce. Because I knew that one day you would return, and I wanted to be free when you did."

Stubbs growled softly, and dropped the stick in front of Penelope, his ultimate compliment.

She took it, saying, "Come on, boy. Let's go for a swim."

Before Mick could say anything, she and Stubbs went down the stairs toward the beach.

He looked down at the beach. It was empty except for Penelope and Stubbs. She beckoned to Mick, then slipped off her white terry cover-up. She walked toward the water with the grace of a woman confident of her beauty.

He smiled. He had come home, at last.

Mick ran down the stairs and headed toward the beach. Then he stopped. He had forgotten something.

He went over to the van and opened the glove compartment,

then put the little box that lay inside it into the pocket of his shorts.

The striped beach towel was spread on the sand near the bluff, hidden behind a group of boulders. Penelope was swimming along the shore with a slow and rhythmic stroke. He had forgotten what a good swimmer she was.

He slipped off his shorts and folded them neatly on the towel, making sure the little box didn't fall out of the pocket. He took off his sandals, then walked to the wet sand at the water's edge and watched the waves, waiting for the right one to come and carry him into the sea.

When that right one came and towered, glassy, emerald green in front of him—its clear crest high and unbroken—Mick dived into it, and swam to meet her.